My Summer Love

Elisabeth Ogilvie

SCHOLASTIC INC.
New York Toronto London Auckland Sydney

ISBN 0-590-33266-X

12 11 10 9 8 7 6 5 4 3 2   5 6 7 8 9/8 0/9

Printed in the U.S.A.   06

My
Summer
Love

A Wildfire Book

One

The first thing I said, when my parents confronted me with the news from my guidance counselor, was "Why?"

"Diana," my father said, "you are the only one who knows why you flunked most of your finals."

I'd just blurted it out, like yelping when you hit your crazy bone or slam a door on your finger. Life had just walloped me on the crazy bone and jammed my whole hand in the door.

But he was right. I was the only one who did it. Or didn't do it. Didn't pass math. Didn't pass Latin. Didn't pass English. Didn't even complete required reading for English. But is there anything worse than knowing you can't blame anybody else? I went on staring piteously at them while I tried to think.

My mother said gently, "Di, Mrs. Dunn says your teachers thought it was enough to talk to you about your math and Latin, instead of sending home warning slips, because you've always been such a good, responsible student. So what *were* you doing up in your room or over at Kim's, or at the library, when you were supposed to be studying?"

"We talked a lot," I said lamely.

"And did Kim pass all her finals?"

"Yes," I said unwillingly. Traitor Kim. She could have at least failed along with me.

"I'm curious," said my father. "What did you talk about?"

"We just talked," I said vaguely. "About everything. You know."

"I *don't* know, and I'm trying to find out what was so important that you could let this happen. Do you realize that you're not going to graduate with your class?"

I realized it, and I wanted to be alone so I could contemplate the awfulness of it. The only way to end this scene was to tell the truth, but leaving out Tom Latimer, who'd been occupying my mind when it should have been concerned most of the time with geometry, literature, and Latin.

So I lifted my chin and said, "I goofed off. I got lazy. I've had good marks all my life and I liked getting them. But all of a sudden this spring they didn't seem that important, compared to real life. I knew I was letting things slide, but I kept thinking I could pull up whenever I wanted to. But time went too fast. I mean, all of a sudden it was time for exams."

They looked at me in silence. Suddenly I had to swallow. "I suppose I've disgraced you. You'll never be able to hold your heads up in public again."

"Oh, for heaven's sake!" said my mother. "It isn't the end of the world!"

"But if there's anything wrong," said my father, "anything disturbing you, we want to know. We care about you."

"I know you do!" I felt tearful. "But I can promise you I'm not — uh — emotionally disturbed except for feeling pretty mad and stupid right now, and I'm not anorectic —"

"Now *that* I'm sure of," said my mother, which broke the tension and produced some weak grins.

"If you're disgusted with me, I'm ten times more disgusted with myself."

I went upstairs and shut myself into my room. Sam, our tiger cat, was on my bed and I fitted myself around him and hugged him to me. I've been hugging him since I was about four. Also crying on him. I cried a little now, but as his rumbling purr began I knew I was forcing the self-pity. I *was* disgusted with myself. How could I have been so *dumb?*

Well, you can call yourself names for just so long. September and school were almost three months away, and the anguish of seeing my friends graduate without me was a whole year away. I had gotten myself a summer job in Latimer's Hardward Store. Tom's father owned it, and Tom worked there all summer. I'd applied for the job in person to Mr. Latimer early in May, and I was going to be with Tom six days a week, and on weekends if I could manage it. And now with school about to end, the job was about to begin.

I'd been lying in the porch hammock happily deciding what I'd wear to work to do the most for my eyes, and what I needed new for those great weekend dates, when Mrs. Dunn had called from school.

I squeezed Sam too hard and he squirmed, so I let him go, skipped over the unpleasant scene downstairs, and returned blissfully to Tom. Terry, his current steady, was going on a bicycle tour of the British Isles. Some of the kids envied her, but not me. She had to leave Tom behind and, from the way he looked at me, I knew that under the right circumstances I could move right in on him.

Who'd have guessed that a hardware store could be as romantic as a moonlit garden?

I bounced off the bed and went to look at myself in my mirror. What did Tom see? I'm moderately tall, not skinny but thin enough to look good in jeans, and I have lots of curly light brown hair which I wish had stayed blonde, as it was when I was small. And sometimes I wish it was straight and sleek. My eyes are blue sometimes, and sometimes more gray. I'd rather have emerald-green or sapphire-blue eyes, or velvety brown eyes with long, curling black lashes. But my eyebrows are pretty without plucking, and I have strong cheekbones and a good dimple in one cheek, which is more provocative than a dimple in each. And nowadays it's okay to have summer freckles on your nose and a little gap between your two front teeth. I mean, I've seen pictures of highly-paid models with these things.

My normal state of mind is optimistic, and being cheerful makes people like to be around you, even if you're not a spectacular beauty. So I've never been lonesome even though I'm an only child.

Even now, after the shock of finding out that my laziness and daydreaming had caught up with me, I was quickly recovering. With Tom I could face anything. I could still go to all the senior affairs, so except for actual classroom hours, and not being allowed to date on school nights, I'd still have plenty of time with Tom and be able to hold the line against Terry when she came back from her bicycle tour.

My heart thumped happily. No need to daydream now that I'd have the reality. So I would work like mad this coming year, and I would ignore snickers of younger kids as I rose above the shame of repeating the grade. I would hold my head high and I would be Tom Latimer's girl.

That girl was smiling confidently at me from the mirror when my mother spoke outside the door.

"May I come in, Di?"

"Mmm." My reflection and I let our mouths droop sadly.

"Well, Di," my mother said briskly, "what's done is done, so instead of looking back we have to make some constructive plans. Mrs. Dunn just called again, and your father and I are very pleased. Your teachers would all like to see you move ahead with your class. So they agreed that if you can make up your work with a tutor this summer, and get all your required reading done, you can take your exams again before school starts."

She beamed at me and I looked blankly at her. Studying wasn't part of my summer plans. Studying was for next year, when I'd really buckle down. But not *now*.

"Mother, I really need the pay from my job!" I exclaimed. "I'm going to put it all straight into my college account." (Except for the first few weeks' pay, which would be spent on a couple of new swimsuits and so forth for my weekends with Tom.) "With interest it'll really count! It'll pay for my first year's books and some extras besides. But if I'm tutored, you and Dad will have to pay, so money will be going out and nothing coming in, don't you see?"

I was inspired; the words just tumbled out. "And it'll do me good to have to repeat. I'll get a firmer grasp on things the second time around, and I —"

I think I overdid it. She didn't say so,

but there's a certain aura they get when they're on to you.

"We think you should go on with your class," she said. "You can take over the mowing and the clipping, and paint the garage, all of which will save us money, and you could always refuse your allowance," she said dryly. "You'll probably have plenty of baby-sitting, too, to help out that bank account. Now run downstairs and talk to Danny. He wants to know what color you'll be wearing to the prom."

Dear, devoted, dull Danny. Thank goodness he was going out west to a baseball camp this summer, so I wouldn't have to hurt his feelings when Tom and I became an item. He'd probably come home in love with a girl shortstop, anyway.

Suddenly the facts burst through my daydreams. I wasn't going to have all that time with Tom! My parents and teachers were going to see to that. Now I really wanted to cry, hard, but I pinned a brave smile on my face and marched downstairs to tell him I'd be wearing Dawn Peach.

With my talent for seeing the bright side, I decided they wouldn't be able to find the right tutor for me, somebody who was strong on both Latin and math. So I didn't rush to tell Mr. Latimer I couldn't take the job. But I acted sufficiently depressed when I was with my parents.

What with all the activities of the last week of school, Kim and I didn't get together for a real talk until the day of the prom. The school year ended at noon and she came to my house for lunch. My mother was in Boston for the day, and Dad was downtown at his insurance office.

Kim is going to be an interior decorator, and I'm going to design all her clothes, and we'll pass our clients on to each other. I have already done some designing and sewing for both Kim and myself, and even for my mother.

So occasionally we would talk about our careers. It wasn't *always* Love and Boys, but it mostly was. Today Kim had a different subject.

"My gosh, I never *dreamed* you were so far behind! Why didn't you cram? I'd have helped you."

"Cramming's no good. You just stuff your brain till you can't think anyway. Listen, it's my fault and I don't want to talk about it any more."

"But you're a good reader, I thought you'd at least get through the reading list." Half the English exam questions had dealt with the reading list.

"I dream too much," I said. "How's that for a good title? Let's write a song and make our fortune."

"I think it's taken," said Kim. "Darn it, Di, we were going to start at the Art Institute together, year after next. Now you probably won't even get in."

"Thanks for the vote of confidence," I said bitterly.

"Tom Latimer will be a college man when you're still a high school kid." She sounded more distressed than mean.

"Don't forget I'll be working with him this summer!"

"You mean you'll be working with that tutor," Kim said.

"They have to find one first. Dad wants to put an ad in the paper, but Mother wants one personally recommended."

"He might be some handsome college student," Kim said, eagerly.

"No such luck. Besides, nobody, but *nobody*, could outclass Tom Latimer. Anyway, Kim," I said with proper solemnity, "I'm resigned to repeating the year. I really feel it would be very good discipline for me."

"Oh, baloney," said Kim. "Don't you even *care* that we won't be starting at the Institute together, after all our plans?"

"Yes, I do care," I said indignantly, "but —"

Suddenly she gave me her impish grin. "Oh well, I don't blame you for wanting to make time with Tom. I know how I felt about Paul. That's what summers are for, at our age. Gather ye roses while we may, and stuff. Tell you what, I'll get a job for a year and wait for you. How's that?"

"Terrific!" I just had to give her a hug, and then we had a good session all about Tom and her Paul, and the things the four of us could do together this summer. I felt so positive, as if nothing could stop me now. I kept seeing Tom, the way he ambled down the corridors as if he weren't quicksilver on the basketball and tennis courts; the way he cocked that fair head and gave me that mischievous wink as if we already shared secrets. And those blue eyes. . . .

To be with him all summer — heaven! It made me almost sick to my stomach with joy.

When my mother came home, Kim had gone, and I was virtuously mowing the lawn. After I finished, Mother had cold drinks set out on the kitchen table for us, and some fancy cookies she'd bought in Boston.

"I had a fabulous day!" she exclaimed. She went on telling me about the very old but restored houses she'd visited. She's into historic preservation; I mean she's an expert. She's paid to do research for people, and towns ask for her advice.

I thought I'd add to her pleasure by showing an interest in the old college friend she'd met for lunch. She lives out in the country, in the western part of the state. I'd never met her, but she and Mother are able to have lunch in Boston several times a year.

"Lunch was as fabulous as the houses," my mother told me now. "I've found a tutor for you, and a nice job in a lovely place. This way you can prepare for your exams and earn your way, but vacation at the same time. You've been so depressed lately, the change will do you good."

If I hadn't been sitting down, I'd have had to. "Where?" I asked numbly. "Who?"

"Madge Thornton is perfectly qualified, and more than willing. She's teaching summer courses at the college out there, and she needs a good responsible sitter for her two younger children so her older boy will be free to take paying jobs. She's a widow, you know, and raising three children on what she makes as an assistant professor means she needs every cent she can get. They live on Hawthorne Farm, the old Thornton homestead. It was built in 1694!" She was starry-eyed. "I've never seen it, but I'm certainly going to, now that you'll be out there!"

My head felt full of dirty wet wool, with a bright blue bit of yarn running through it. Bright blue like Tom Latimer's eyes.

"You are going to love it," she told me. "I know *I* would!"

Of course she didn't know about Tom. Only Kim knew. And if I told her this was my one chance at the golden prize, would she agree I should take it? No. Parents are so darned *practical*. She'd say I couldn't be sure Tom would fall for me, but I could be sure of the tutoring. *That*'s what I needed, and that's what I'd get.

"You looked stunned," my mother said, smiling. "It must be a tremendous relief to know you can go on with your class."

"Mother," I said, trying not to panic, "the job at Latimer Hardware pays real money and I think I need it as much as that boy needs his. And I'm resigned to repeating the year, I really am." I bravely lifted my chin. "I know I'll feel awful, but I deserve it. I goofed off, and now I have to face the consequences. You know how you and Dad always say people have to take responsibility for their own actions. Well, that's what I'm going to do."

"Making up the work is what counts." She patted my arm. "And the way you've faced up to your behavior really pleases your father and me. We think you deserve a chance to go ahead with your class."

"You've already talked it over with *him*?" I yelped.

"Yes. I stopped by the office on my way home. He's as pleased as I am."

"I can't believe you'd commit me to this without talking to me about it first." Darn it, my eyes were filling up. "I mean, I'm practically an adult, and —"

"Darling, I had to make a quick decision, and I knew that you were sunk about staying behind your class."

"But why should Mrs. Thornton trust me with her children? I could be awful."

"She knows no daughter of mine could be awful. She knows that if I say you're sensible and an experienced sitter with a talent for kids, then that's what you are. Just as I know that after a summer of her tutoring you'll pass those exams like a whiz kid. Now, how about steaks and strawberry shortcake for dinner tonight?"

T*wo*

That was the worse prom I'd ever attended. For me, I mean. Not that anybody knew it, because I can be quite a heroine when I try: dancing with a smile on my lips when I know that on the stroke of midnight I'm going to turn into a pumpkin, and the prince wouldn't even miss me.

He and Terry spent the evening swooning into each other's eyes. Kim and Paul and Danny and I always hung together at dances, and I was putting on such a great performance that even Kim didn't suspect disaster. Danny, of course, wouldn't notice anything unless I was raining tears and choking with loud sobs. He was a good kid and I appreciated that; we went together because neither of us wanted to be seriously committed. That is, I hadn't wanted to be until I set my heart on Tom Latimer and knew I had a chance.

I wasn't able to tell Kim anything until the

next day when we got together at her house to talk over the prom. On the way there I'd stopped at the hardware store and told Mr. Latimer I couldn't take the job.

"Thank goodness Tom wasn't there," I told Kim. "I'd have died on the spot. And it would have been a relief, the way I feel."

"You overdid all that remorse and woe about staying behind," Kim said. "Where did you say this place was?"

"I don't know. I don't care. I just know I hate it. I'll bet Carol Harper is on the job already; she was next on the list."

"Don't worry about her," Kim said. "She's not Tom's type at all. Oh, he'll be nice, because he's always the charm boy, but for dating he'd never give her a second look."

"He won't be giving me any second looks either," I said gloomily. "Kim, I can't *bear* it!"

She observed a reverent silence for a moment and then said, "I'll keep you informed."

"Thanks, but I don't know if I want to be."

My parents thought I was long-faced from premature homesickness.

"Look at this as an adventure," my father told me. "You're going out into the world to meet new people and new experiences. We're only a telephone call away, but don't overdo that. Call us once a week and reverse the charges. In between you can write us letters."

My allowance would be sent me, but there was nothing to spend it on in the wilderness.

Right then I decided to blow it all on telephone calls to confide in Kim.

One sparkling June morning I dressed in my lilac suit and frilly blouse strewn with violets, kissed the top of Sam's head, and rode with my mother to the Greyhound station. Taking the bus was my idea; I didn't want to be delivered like a little kid.

As the bus drove away I felt as if I were living one of those Gothic novels I loved to read. I was the orphaned and penniless girl setting out by stagecoach to be a governess in a weird old mansion built on a lonely moor, or perched on a cliff above the sea. Out on the moors the wolves would howl, and from the cliff there would always be the thunder of the surf and the lonely cries of gulls. Inside the mansion, mysterious staircases led to locked doors with strange noises behind them. There's be an old servant who went around shaking his or her head and muttering warnings.

By afternoon we were in the real country, with steep green hills, woods, and streams. Cows and horses watched us over pasture fences, and once I saw a field of sheep with lambs. I saw neat farmhouses set back from the highway under big trees. Some of them were really beautiful, and in one driveway there were some small children on ponies and a couple of older girls on horses. They all looked rich and confident.

Until now Hawthorne Farm had simply been the place of my exile. But now a new *me* took over the timid Gothic heroine. If I'd lost my one chance with Tom Latimer, I was going out into the world, as Dad said, and it could be exciting, apart from the studying and the kids. They needn't be too bad either. They were six and eight, and probably had their own ponies. There'd be horses, too, and I could learn how to ride.

Now Mrs. Thornton's older son, who'd been a nonentity so far, really came alive, a bronzed, long-legged, outdoor type wearing Levis and a turtleneck. The 17th-century farmhouse became one of those grand white houses under the elms.

My stomach was improving all the time. "Thank you, Mother," I murmured to the blue-tinted window. I could hardly wait to arrive.

In mid-afternoon we drove into the small town of Barclay. With its tree-shaded main street, it was as pretty as a magazine cover. There was a short business block, and the bus halted outside the row of diagonally parked cars. I was the only person getting off, and I walked behind the driver as he carried my two bags to the sidewalk between a Mercedes and a shabby old pickup truck. A mostly German shepherd dog stood in the back of it and barked at us. He was huge and he had an enormous bark, and looked as if he should be guarding prisoners in one of those war movies I hate. I made a leap for the sidewalk where I could be defended by the driver and the men sitting on the bench outside the drugstore. I hoped that the dogs at Hawthorne Farm were all lovable, like Irish setters.

Two women came along to board the bus and I was left standing on the sidewalk in this strange town, pleasantly ignored by the passersby, who were so comfortably at home. Only that dog knew I existed, and he stared unnervingly at me from the truck. How soon before he leaped? Sweat trickled down my back. Where were the people from Hawthorne Farm? Was there a mix-up in the dates? In five more minutes I was going to find a telephone and call home. That is, if I dared turn my back on that monster.

Suddenly the dog flattened his ears, his eyes changed, and he was waving his tail. At *me*? No. Someone coming out of the drugstore; he must have been watching that door all the time, not me. I loosened my grip on my pocketbook, took a welcome deep breath, and watched the three kids cross the sidewalk.

The older boy was short and stocky, with crow-black hair. He wore old bib overalls smeared with paint over a shirt with the sleeves ripped off at the shoulders, and he was very tanned. He was carrying three ice-cream cones. The two small kids, in shorts and jerseys, scurried ahead of him and climbed into the back of the pickup. The dog looked as if he were going to eat them. The older boy handed up the cones, two of them to the skinny dark little boy, who began licking the drip first off one and then the other.

"You pig!" the plump little blonde girl cried. "That one's Walter's!"

Walter had to be Monster-Dog. At the sound of his name he lunged forward and his huge tongue came out and began licking the vanilla cone.

"Now you kids *sit* and stay *sat*," Overalls said sternly. He came around to the sidewalk and confronted me. "Are you Diana Moore?" His eyes were clear green with black lashes.

"Yes," I said, managing a gracious smile. Maybe he was just someone who worked at the farm, and Mrs. Thornton's son was at home exercising the horses or something.

"I'm Mac Thornton." His tone said, *You wanna make something of it?*

"Hi," I said weakly.

As he reached for my bags, one of the men on the bench said, "You got you a pretty one, Mac."

He scowled, and the men chuckled. He put my bags in the back of the truck. The kids licked their ice cream and stared at me as Monster-Dog had done; *he* was busy crunching down the last of his cone. The boy's eyes were dark and unblinking, the girl had round blue eyes, also unwavering. I'm an experienced sitter and I've met up with enough new clients not to panic while they sized me up, but all I could think was, *Are these two going to be little horrors?*

Mac opened the door for me and I climbed in. I didn't see much of the scenery on the ride out to the farm, I just stared at the road ahead. The hostility in the cab was all but smothering me.

Suddenly the truck turned left off the highway, by a mailbox, and we trundled noisily along a narrow dirt road that went up and down and around, through woods and past overgrown fields where there were no glossy horses, no cute sheep and lambs, no sleek cows that promised real cream on the cereal.

We seemed to go on forever, with my stomach getting sicker and sicker, until we came to a rise and I saw blue water through the pines on the bank below.

Then the truck went down the slope to the left and the first thing I saw was the barn, because it was so big. And then, over to the right, the house.

It was small and low, shabby and gray, huddled under two big maples like a scared cat under the bushes. This must be the place where the farm manager lived, the foreman or whatever they called him. The 17th-century treasure of a house and the rich fields of crops and livestock had to be somewhere beyond that circling wall of forest.

I was still telling myself this when the truck stopped in front of the barn. The kids climbed out over the tailgate, and Monster-Dog took a flying leap to the ground and was waiting to eat me.

"Does that dog bite?" I asked.

"He won't bite you." Mac Thornton

sounded bored. Halfway out of the truck seat, with Walter lumbering around and panting as if my first foot out would make him a nice hors d'oeuvre, and the kids like ancient Romans waiting to see the Christians thrown to the lions, I blurted out, "Listen, this wasn't *my* idea!"

"Yeah? Well, it wasn't mine either. But I've got to work for money that I can't afford to turn down. Roger, get the wheelbarrow!" he yelled and Roger rushed off toward the house.

Well, Mother's old friend would make me feel welcome even if her kids hated me on sight. I gathered my courage and stepped down. Walter rushed at me, I held my breath, and he pranced around me like a setter pup wanting you to chase him. Tail going like mad. I extended my fist and he smelled it all over, licked it, and then looked into my eyes and gave me a lovely dog smile.

I breathed naturally again; at least the dog liked me. The little girl stood staring at us with saucer eyes, her lips tight in her round face. Roger came rushing back with a big wooden wheelbarrow, making engine noises. Mac loaded a box of groceries and my bags into the wheelbarrow, and Walter frisked around. The girl's round blue eyes never left me.

"Tabby, take this." Roger handed her a paper bag. Barn swallows came swooping low over our heads and dive-bombed two cats, one white and one black, who'd come to meet the family. There was the scent of country air, and the fragrance of the bright untidy masses of flowers around the gray old house. I was trying desperately not to be swamped by my despair. *Remember you're a Gothic heroine*, I told myself. *Chin up! You're all alone in the world and you have to make your own way in it.*

My reward for that was the old servant in the kitchen. She was just like in the books, except that she wasn't old, just not young, and she didn't call the kids Masters Mac and Roger and Miss Tabby. But if they had *her*, why did they need me?

She gave me a sharp glance and went on with her work. The action swirled around her like a whirlpool as all the Thorntons put the food away. It was very noisy and I felt more of an alien than ever.

Finally the noise stopped and Mac said ungraciously, "Mrs. Hill, this is Diana Moore. Diana, Mrs. Hill."

"How do you do, Mrs. Hill?" I was gracious. "Everyone calls me Di."

She nodded. "Hello."

"Any telephone calls?" Mac asked her.

"Nope. It's likely too early yet." She slid a pan of bread dough into the oven.

"They're probably having a big family re-union first," Mac said with a bitter twist to his mouth.

He took my bags and went through a narrow door in a corner of the kitchen beyond this huge old brick fireplace that would have put my mother out of her mind with joy. The door opened onto a narrow, twisting staircase, and then I heard him walking overhead.

"You young ones show her to her room," said Mrs. Hill.

Not Diana, not Di. Just *her*. Where was the telephone? I could hear myself wailing over it to my mother, *I shouldn't have come, they all hate me*!

I decided against it, knowing full well my mother would tell me to wait a week and see how I felt then. Well, I knew how I'd feel, but I'd wait out the week. Where was Mrs. Thornton, who, according to my mother, was such a dear? I doubted that even she could make up for the rest of them.

Without a word the kids led me into the front hall, up the steep front stairs and to a corner room with a slanting ceiling. I looked all around me, and the two watched me.

"Where's your mother?" I asked.

Roger raised his eyebrows and shrugged his shoulders. Tabby just stared at me.

"Well, you can at least point to the bathroom," I said coldly.

*T*hree

It was a plain, old-fashioned bathroom, but there were plenty of towels and hot water. I washed up and combed my hair, and when I went back to my room the kids were gone. Next to my room a door stood open into what was plainly Tabby's room. Across the narrow hall from us another door was open into what had to be Mac's room, a big one on the back of the house.

My room was furnished very simply with old pieces that would have had my mother in rapture. There was a good reading light, and the bed felt comfortable when I sat on it. Not that it mattered much to me — I was too depressed. The only thing that helped me was the determination to get away from here as soon as possible, even if I had to throw myself on the mercy of my parents. I'd wait a week before I abased myself, but I was darned sure I was going to do it.

My side window, under the slanting ceiling, looked past the kitchen wing toward the big barn, the green meadow beyond it, and then those grim dark woods. The front window looked out past the big maples to the road that would seem like heaven to me when I was on it, going *out*. By pressing my cheek against the screen, I could get a glimpse of the bright blue lake through the pines.

Birds were singing everywhere, but though I like birds as well as anyone they didn't do anything for me now. I changed into denim shorts and a sleeveless blouse, and went out to the main hall. There were two doors on the other side of the stairs. One was closed, and one was open. All the doors I'd seen so far had these old-fashioned thumb latches, another thrill for my mother. I wished gloomily that she had this job instead of me.

When I went down the stairs, I saw the telephone on a table in the lower hall. A grandfather clock ticked loudly against the wall. I found my way to the kitchen through a cluttered dining room, which had papers and books piled on the table, and a small TV in one corner. Mrs. Hill was taking bread from the oven.

She gave me this steely look. "You had any lunch?" (Accusingly, like *Did you rob the bank?*)

"Yes." I told her where we'd stopped and she sniffed.

"*That* place. Burned hamburgers and stale sandwiches. Here." She handed me a glass, and nodded at the refrigerator. "Help yourself to milk. Will bread and butter do you till dinner tonight?"

"Oh yes!" I was grateful because she was talking to me.

"Get out the butter then. Silver in this drawer. I'll cut the bread, you're likely to chop off a finger."

Homemade bread sliced off the loaf! I couldn't have been happier.

"There's nothing like plain bread and butter," I said, "if it's good bread like this. Where's Mrs. Thornton?" I tried to be casual. "She's an old friend of my mother's, and she was going to be here, I thought."

"She had to go away suddenly." The words were snapped off. "It's an emergency. She got the word late last night."

"Oh no, I hope nobody's sick!"

"No. She'll be back in a couple of days."

"If you're here, Mrs. Hill," I said respectfully, "why do they need a sitter? Roger and Tabby obey you, and they sure don't want *me*."

"Making no bones about it, are they?"

"They haven't spoken to me yet, and Mac just says what he has to. Well, Walter is friendly anyway." I tried to laugh. "I don't know about the cats."

"Inkie and Snow will like you fine. The rest of 'em will just have to put up with you," she said. "I'm only here to look out for things while Mrs. Thornton is away. Fact is, if you weren't here Mac would be in charge. He's a real capable boy. But with a young girl here, there ought to be a chaperone in the house." She gave me a sidewise glance over her glasses. "You know what those are?"

"Sure. We have them at the dances and on school trips. Sometimes my parents are chaperones."

"Oh. Thought they might've gone out of date in the city."

I felt like saying, *If you think Mac and I fell in love at first sight and need watching, you've got another think coming. My heart is back in Latimer's Hardware, palpitating among the no-stick frying pans.*

"Mrs. Hill, will you tell me something about the children?" I asked.

"When you get acquainted," she said, "then you'll know." Which was no help at all. I was going to be alone with those two all day out here in this wilderness. And when their mother and brother came home, if I wasn't exhausted, what was there for fun? I'd probably be expected to go to bed when it was dark under the table, as my grandmother put it, and be up with the birds.

"Well," I said sadly, "I guess I'd better unpack. Thank you for lunch. It was great." *I'll unpack for just one week,* I promised myself.

I rinsed my glass with cold water to show how well-trained I was, and put away the butter.

"You're welcome," she said, probably pitying me. What horrors did she know of those two?

Drearily I went through the cluttered dining room, and peeked in at a library-study. All those books! Across the hall, the living room was shabby but comfortable, with its end windows looking down at the lake. There were fireplaces in all the downstairs rooms, and they all looked used. Behind the living room through a partly open door I glimpsed a pleasant bedroom that must have been Mrs. Thornton's.

When would Mrs. Thornton be back? I could imagine her arriving home just as I was about to leave.

I went out the front door and sat on the brick doorstep between the pink and red climbing roses. The white cat came from somewhere and leaned against my legs, purring. I missed Sam like mad. "Hello, Snow," I said, and then I heard them coming around the barn before I saw them. Tabby was riding Mac's shoulders, and Roger was galloping ahead, waving this big wooden sword. Walter was poking along, unconcerned about the noise, and the black cat followed, tail straight in the air.

Mac, laughing, was somebody different from the sour character who'd met me in town, but not for long. As soon as they saw me they stopped as if I were the Black Death. But Walter was charming.

Mac hunched down for Tabby to dismount. "All right, you kids," he said. "I have to take Mrs. Hill home so she can make supper for her family, and I'll take Walter along to get his booster shots at the vet's. Behave yourselves."

"We want to go with you!" Tabby whined.

"Yeah!" Roger joined in.

So I'd be left alone miles from everywhere, and who knew what was in those woods all around?

"No, you stay with *her*. Start getting acquainted. Why don't you show her around?"

I felt like saying, "The name is Diana," but I didn't. He went in the back door, and they rushed in after him. Walter went, too, and Snow decided to follow Inkie to the source of food.

I shut myself up in my room and unpacked. I waited until the truck rattled out with Mrs. Hill and Walter aboard, waited a few minutes more, and then went downstairs.

Tabby sat alone on the front doorsteps, hugging Inkie. She looked very sad. I smiled at her. "What are you going to show me first?"

"Roger ran away," she said starkly. "He's never coming back. Because he hates you."

My legs went weak. "But why?" I asked. "I never did anything to him!"

"It's because you're here," she explained serenely, "and we don't want you. We want our brother."

"Your brother has to work," I began, and than panic hit. *He ran away while you're in*

*charge, Di. And you're miles from home and
don't know a soul.* "Which way did he go?"
I snapped. "To the lake? To the road?"

She tucked in her lips, put her fingers to
them and turned an imaginary key. I felt
like shaking her. I put my hands to my
mouth and yelled "Roger!" as loud as I could.
My echo came back from the woods. Tabby
sat motionless on the doorstep. *Smug* was
the word.

"You'd better tell me which way he went,
Tabitha Thornton," I said coldly, "because
when I call the police they have to be told."

"Well," she said, "he *was* going on his
bike, but we aren't allowed on the main road,
only as far as the mailbox." She stopped.

"So which way did he go?" My hands
itched to take hold of her. "All right, don't
answer! I'll catch Mac either at Mrs. Hill's or
the vet's."

She blinked rapidly. "He went on the old
road in the woods. It goes all the way to
Barclay. He took his sleeping bag and some
food for tonight." She sounded both proud
and envious.

"Come on!" I grabbed her hand. "We're
going to find him. You can show me the
way."

"I don't want to!" She shrank into a pite-
ous little bundle. "We aren't supposed to go
into the woods!"

"But if there's a road, we can't get lost.
Come on!" I pulled her up, and she whim-
pered. "Or do you want me to call the police

29

first? And *Mac*?" That was shrewd; she suddenly became cooperative, and led me around the house into an old orchard, and through it toward the woods.

These were really deep woods, unlike the tame groves around home. Just a few yards into them along the old track, I couldn't see anything but woods behind me. The orchard and the ancient house had disappeared off the face of the earth.

*F*our

I kept a good grip on Tabby's hand. It was so quiet and gloomy in here, it took courage for me to keep calling, as if I'd wake up a lot more than echoes. Once some crows suddenly took off from overhead, making me almost jump out of my skin.

"Roger took his cap pistol to scare off the wolves," Tabby remarked.

"Wolves?" My voice went into a squeak.

"Roger's brave," she said proudly. "He says if you keep a campfire going all night they won't come near you. So he took matches, too."

My heart was pounding. Did I dare go any farther? Should I rush back and call the police? But what about the little boy with his cap pistol to scare off the wolves? And *matches*? He might be just ahead of me.

I swallowed several times to moisten my throat so I could yell again. I put my hands to my mouth to shout, and of course I had to let go of Tabby.

She was there one instant, gone the next. I stood peering all around me. It all looked blind to me. The track could have been anywhere across the brown needles under the tall spruces. Anywhere or nowhere, just like Tabby. My throat shut tight. I couldn't have called her, and she wouldn't have answered if I had.

"Be calm, be calm, Diana," I whispered. "*Think.* Where is the sun?" But it was so shadowy in here, the branches so thick overhead, the sun would be no help. "Don't move from this spot," I commanded myself. "Hunters get lost because they start going in circles. Sit down and somebody will come for you after a while."

Unless Roger was hiding in the barn all the time, said a horrid little voice in my head, *and Tabby was supposed to lose you out here. They'll tell Mac they haven't seen you since he drove out. So nobody will ever know where you went, or what happened to you, until your bones are found, years from now.*

If wolves leave *bones,* said an even more horrid voice. *You've got to get yourself out of here.*

Didn't I know *that* tree? Hadn't we come by it? I took a few more steps, wasn't sure, took a few more. Had we come through this open spot?

"Tabby!" I shouted. "Roger!" Only echoes

mocked me, and then as they died away I heard something else.

The howl of a wolf.

I'd heard wolf howls on a record once and thought they were beautiful. But not now. I knew what a cold sweat was. How close had that howl been? Was it a signal to the pack? Were they even now padding silently through the woods to surround me?

Something was coming. My sweaty hands fumbled around on the ground for a fallen rock. Through low branches I saw flashes of white and gray and brown as it came. I found a rock as big as my head, and held it before me, knowing I had only one chance to hurl it.

The wolf trotted out into the open. It grinned fiercely as it saw its prey. It stopped to savor the moment, pointed its muzzle toward the sky, and howled again. Then it bounded toward me wagging its tail. It was Walter.

I dropped my rock, just missing my foot. Weakly I knelt and embraced my only friend at Hawthorne Farm.

Walter tried to kiss my ear, and I felt like abandoning all pride and bawling into his thick ruff.

Suddenly Mac's voice was battering me. "What's the idea of leaving these kids and going off on your own and getting lost? Tabby was scared to death!"

Kneeling by Walter, I looked up at them. Tabby was on his shoulders. His green eyes accused; his cheeks were flushed with rage.

Over his head her blue eyes were round, her lips locked, trying not to grin in triumph. All at once I was calm.

"What did she tell you?" I stood up.

"You wanted to take a walk into the woods, and she told you they aren't supposed to go, so you went anyway. She said Roger was trying to find you. And where the heck is *he*?" He glared around the clearing. "It's a good thing Walter heard you yell. Otherwise you could have been here all night." *And good enough for you*, his expression said.

"Then Roger and I could have kept each other company," I retorted. "If I could find him. We'd do all right. I hear he's got his cap pistol and some food and his sleeping bag. *And* matches."

"What do you mean?" He jerked his head irritably. "Tabby, stop pulling my hair! What's this about Roger?"

"He ran away just as soon as you drove out, I guess. Before I came downstairs. Tabby told me. She says he hates me so he's not staying. She said he was going through the woods along an old track to some place, and I wanted to see if he'd gone very far before I called the police."

His face changed from icy disapproval to angry bewilderment, which gave way to a grim tight smile. All right, so he didn't believe me. I'd be away from Hawthorne Farm by nightfall.

"Tabby brought me this far," I went on,

"and when I turned my back for a minute, calling Roger, she ran away."

"And I met her high-tailing across the orchard with her tale of woe," he said. "With tears, yet. I think I'll put her in the movies. She could make a fortune."

He lifted her off his shoulders and set her on the ground. Her mouth was tighter than ever and she was blinking fast.

Walter woofed enthusiastically from behind a tree and then backed into view, tail wagging energetically. He was pulling on something.

Something was the back of Roger's jersey, and Roger was in it. He had no sleeping bag, no food, but he was wearing a cowboy gun belt with twin pistols in flashy holsters.

"It's obvious that this isn't going to work," I said.

"Why?" Mac asked. "This is only the first day."

"And it's been about a year long," I said. "They resent me. I accept that as a fact of life."

"You're a fact of life they'll have to accept," he said tightly. "Like a lot of things. I'll give them a good talking-to tonight. Look, I'll be gone from five-thirty in the morning till about three-thirty or four in the afternoon. I'll leave a number where you can get me if you have to."

"You make them sound dangerous." I tried for a light touch. But he was grim.

"Not dangerous. Just fighting against circumstances. Like the rest of us," he added softly, as if he were thinking aloud.

Out of the woods, the kids raced across the orchard. "Go to your rooms!" Mac called after them. "I'll be up and we'll have a talk!"

"Wait a minute," I said, stopping under a gnarled old apple tree. "You said they're fighting against circumstances. Well, I'm one of the circumstances, and if Roger was really desperate enough to run away, maybe you shouldn't come down on him like a ton of bricks."

"Roger wasn't running away. It was a put-up job, and they won't get away with it."

"But before you talk to them, think why they did it. You said yourself there's an emergency, so here's your mother going off in a hurry, and then this stranger coming in. It upset them. I don't like sudden changes either! Do you know how suddenly this was cooked up for *me*?" I asked feverently.

"Yeah, I guess it was sudden for me, too," he admitted. "Sure, we needed a sitter so I could work. I've got three houses to paint this summer and maybe more. But I thought it would be one of the local girls. Then my mother sprang this new deal on me."

"But *you* know why. Roger and Tabby don't. So please don't be too rough with them or it'll just make my job harder."

He didn't answer that. We were almost at the house. "Are there really wolves?" I asked him, and at that he almost grinned.

"Nope. I wouldn't mind, though. They'd never bother us if we never bothered them."

But I could picture wolves prowling around the house at night, sniffing at our footsteps, watching the lighted windows and looking in at us — well, downstairs, anyway — and I was thankful there were none . . . unless Mac thought I was a Nervous Nellie and couldn't bear to hear the truth. Bears? I wanted to ask about *them*, but I felt foolish enough already.

Mac went straight upstairs and I sat on a step and gazed longingly at the telephone. I could hear his voice, not his words, from Roger's room overhead. He wasn't speaking loudly, but he was steady. I should wait until after five, when the rates changed, to call home. Besides, my mother might be out for the afternoon. But boy, was it hard to wait!

In a little while I heard them all coming downstairs. The kids were very subdued, and smelled of soap and water. Mac had changed from his paint-smudged overalls into a clean, green T-shirt and jeans.

"Roger and Tabby have something to say to you," he said sternly.

I remembered having to apologize to somebody older, and I wanted to make it easy for them, but not too easy. So I tried for the right expression, whatever that was.

"I'm sorry for what I did," Roger said rapidly. "It was wrong."

"I accept your apology," I said graciously. Tabby had her lips locked again.

"Tabby," said Mac. Silence. Then Roger whispered in her ear, and without any change of expression she said to me, "I'm sorry I told you lies and ran away from you in the woods."

"I accept your apology." I was still gracious. Then they went charging out.

"I wonder what he told her," I said. "Probably 'Say you're sorry and tonight we'll blow up her bed.' "

"All we can do is wait and see," he said, and left me. I looked at the pictures in the living room while I waited for five o'clock. Then I waited until five after five to call, but nobody answered. Not at ten after five, either. Obviously my mother didn't expect to hear from me until after dinner. Maybe she and my father were going out somewhere to eat. Little did they care how I might be suffering.

I didn't have long for self-pity because Roger came and told me supper was ready. We ate at the kitchen table. Mrs. Hill had left a big bowl of chicken salad, and we had the homemade bread with it, and cookies and ice cream afterward. The Thorntons were all good eaters; even Tabby cleaned up her plate. And my woe didn't spoil my appetite. I didn't try to take part in the conversation, knowing I'd be unwelcome. I just ate. And ate.

Afterwards I offered to do the dishes, but Mac refused, which is a great way to make a person feel out of it. "There's only a few, and I'll do them. You kids go do your chores now."

"I guess I'll go call home," I said. I felt like adding, "I'm just going to give them the news that they can meet me at the bus stop tomorrow afternoon," but I kept quiet.

My parents weren't home! Well, if I had to keep trying every hour, I would. I couldn't sleep tonight without making that call. Discouraged, I went upstairs. It looked beautiful outdoors, but what was there for *me*? I could sit on the doorstep by the roses, or in one of the swings hanging from the maples, or walk down to the lake. It was still bright enough out not to be scary. But I was too proud to wander around like a lost and unwelcome soul.

After a few minutes of fidgeting, I left my room to call home again, but when I reached the head of the stairs, Mac was sitting on a lower one, talking on the telephone. I could look down on his black head and blocky shoulders, but he didn't know I was there.

"Everything's all right here," he said. "Don't worry. What about up there?" Pause. Then, in a slow, weary way, "Yeah. We're always outnumbered. I sure know how the Indians felt! I'd like to collect a few scalps myself."

Then he said, "Oh, she's outside someplace. I'll tell her you said 'welcome' and all that stuff." *Her*. Old No-Name. Just for that I was about to yell down to him that I was right there and would like a word with his mother, but for some reason I didn't want to tell her over the phone that I was quitting.

"They're putting the chickens in," he went on. "They should be about through. Hang on, and I'll go get them."

He put the telephone down, and went out the front door. I went back along the little hallway between his room and mine. Through the open windows I could hear him whistling to the kids. I lifted the latch of the door into the space over the kitchen, and let myself through. It was a long attic running the length of the kitchen and woodshed downstairs, and there was a cleared space in the middle where an electric train was set up. There were other toys, too, and in one corner Tabby must have played house. Unhappy as I was, I couldn't help thinking this was a nice place on rainy days.

They came into the kitchen beneath me, eager to talk to their mother. I went down the back stairs, and slipped across the kitchen and out while they were running into the front hall. I went out around the back of the house so nobody would see me, and then toward the lake.

The tall straight pines closed in behind me and the house vanished. But ahead the lake glimmered a pale, ghostly blue between the dark trunks.

Five

There was a canoe there, pulled up on the sand and turned over. A little dock jutted out into the lake with a small rowboat hitched to the end. I went and sat on the end, took my sneakers off, and let my feet dangle in the water. It wasn't very cold, and I began to feel more peaceful. The pines smelled good. The birds sang, some of them very sweetly, and now and then a fish came to the surface. The barn swallows swooped low over the surface, catching insects.

Little by little the blue faded. Across the lake you couldn't tell where the shore was, because the dense woods there and their reflection were all one black mass.

Suddenly the hush was shattered by peals of hysterical laughter. They came again and again, filling the twilight with horror. They seemed to be all around me, echoing wildly back and forth. I slammed my hands over my ears, snatched my feet out of the water before something could grab them, and huddled myself into as small a package as possible. But I couldn't shut out that insane laughter, and I was staring around me like a wild thing.

At the house they thought I was still in my room. No one would think to check, or care. I could crouch here all night in this waking nightmare — if I survived.

I had to get onto my feet and out of here. If I ran, it might attract the attention of whatever it was, if it wasn't watching me already. If I was too slow, I'd make an easy target. I rammed my wet feet into sneakers and tiptoed off the dock and across the sand. Over to my right some low black shadows hurried off into the ferns. Wildcats? Panthers? I hadn't thought of *them* before. They were too small to be bears, anyway.

All the time the maniacal laughter went on. I found the path and started up it. It was dark all right, but not black-dark, and the sky was still pale. As long as it was open over my head, I knew I was on the path. So I kept looking up at it, and I put my fingers in my ears to try to blot out that fiendish mirth, which is why I neither heard nor saw anything else until I walked slam bang into something. I let out a terrified yelp, and nearly fell backward down the path.

The object grabbed me roughly by the arms and steadied me. I recognized with relief that it was Mac.

"For Pete's sake! I thought you ran away, too!" he said.

"I was thinking about it," I said bitterly, "but I guess I'll wait for daylight. . . . What's *that*?" I nearly clutched at him as the lunatic hilarity began again.

"Loons," he said.

"What are they, and what are they *doing*?"

"They're birds, and they're just communicating." He was contemptuous of my ignorance. "You're really a city slicker, aren't you?"

I couldn't think of a withering reply to that, so I walked away from him up the path, tripping now and then on my shoelaces. He came behind me, saying, "We think it's pretty musical. They have a long call note, too. I like to hear it, it makes you think you're in a real wilderness. They nest in a secret place along the shore somewhere. The lake belongs to them." He spoke very quietly. "But I don't know for how long."

Something about his quietness reached me. "What do you mean?"

"Nothing." He was surly again. And again I had that sense of being an intruder. Not because the kids didn't like me, but because something had happened since Mrs. Thornton and my mother hatched their plan. Now I was just a nuisance, but they didn't know what to do about it.

Well, *I* did.

As we came out into the open, we heard a car coming, and Mac said, "Johnny Hill's bringing his mother back. You can hear that thing of his a mile away."

"Around here you can hear anything a mile away. A pin dropping." I longed for my street at home. Oh, lovely, busy, home!

The Hill car was noisy enough to drown out the loons as it came down the last grade and clattered into the yard. I heard Walter greet Mrs. Hill and the car turned around and went right out again, with a jaunty toot of its horn. I headed fast for those lighted windows.

"I'll be out of your way tomorrow," I said over my shoulder. No answer. No Mac. He'd disappeared into the night. "Oh well, I'll let you be surprised," I said loudly. "You'll think it's Christmas again when I ask you to take me to the bus, as soon as you get home from work tomorrow."

I went into the kitchen and Mrs. Hill nodded at me. "You just missed your mother. Telephone was ringing when I came in. I told her you and Mac were taking a walk. She sent you her love and says call around six tomorrow night, she'll be waiting."

"Thank you, Mrs. Hill," I said warmly. Little did my mother guess that I'd be on my way home tomorrow night. And I was saved an argument tonight.

I took a shower and got into bed. The loons had shut up, but I thought the silence would keep me awake; you have to experience that deep-country silence to know what it's like. Tomorrow night I'd be sleeping in my own bed, and the next day I'd find a job. I'd lost the Latimer one, but I'd find *something*.

I was just beginning to float when I heard a low voice down by the kitchen door. Instantly I was wide awake. I slid out of bed and tiptoed across the wide floorboards to the side window, knelt by it, and strained to hear. I couldn't see anything because the kitchen lights were out, but it was Mac's voice down there. I couldn't make out the words, but the tone was friendly, even affectionate; sometimes questioning, sometimes reassuring, and once I thought I heard a soft chuckle. From *Mac*?

I couldn't hear another voice, but whoever that person was, she needed an awful lot of reassurance. I decided he had a girl, and maybe he'd wanted her to have the sitter's job, or their parents disapproved of the romance so they had to meet secretly, and she'd come on her bike tonight. Maybe she was worried about *me*. I wished I could call down to her and say, "Don't worry, chum, I wouldn't have him as a gift."

But with all the room around here why, for heaven's sake, did they pick out the back doorstep for a conference, right under my nose? They could have been out in the barn, or the orchard, or down at the lake with his precious loons.

Pretty soon the meeting was over. At least I realized I wasn't hearing anything more. He'd probably walk all the way out to the road with her. Or maybe they had used the old road through the woods.

I crawled back into bed wide awake, and had to read a chapter of *A Tale of Two Cities* to get sleepy again. Then I slept well.

When I woke up the sun was coming into my room, and a rooster was crowing out in the henhouse. I'd slept hard. Since this was my last day here, I felt fine. I could even look out and think what a beautiful day it was, and how the dew flashed like diamonds on the grass, and the birds sang so sweetly, and the barn swallows were like wonderful skaters on air.

Mrs. Hill went out to the pickup.

Mac came out in his painting overalls, carrying a lunch box, and walked briskly to his pickup. I wondered what his girl looked like. Knowing about her, I felt kindly toward him this morning.

"How about giving me a tour of the place?" I suggested to the kids at breakfast. "You know everything about the country and I don't, so how about it?"

Roger couldn't resist this. "Sure," he said gruffly. "Come on." We started for the door and Tabby followed quickly. We rambled for hours, and I felt good because we'd used up so much of the day and I was getting close to departure time. I could also see that Hawthorne Farm was a wonderful place for those who had grown up here, even though I was glad to be leaving.

S^{ix}

I had promised the kids we would have our lunch by the lake that day. When I came downstairs with my beach towel draped over a black and white swimsuit originally intended to dazzle Tom Latimer, the kids were trying to assemble a lunch on the kitchen table.

I made sandwiches, and I helped them put the milk, cookies, and bananas they had laid out into a canvas bag which I slung over my shoulder as we headed for the lake.

In sunlight, the lake was like a blue gem, all twinkling. There was an old picnic table where we left our food in the shade, and the cats sat beside it on guard.

I didn't try any long distance swimming, just swam back and forth about twenty feet out, while the kids stayed between the shore and me. They were good little swimmers, real water babies, and we all laughed and splashed together, and it was really nice. Water does that for you, if you like it.

Afterward we carried our lunch to the little dock. Seated on the warm planks, we ate and drank, passing out bits to the animals. "We can't ever do that when we're at the table," Tabby said happily.

"And we can't ever come to the lake, even just to play and eat, unless some older person is with us," Roger said.

"So now we can do it every day," said Tabby.

"Do they call you Di, like that princess?" Roger asked me.

"Yep," I said. I had a twinge of guilt and regret. Right now I felt really good. But I knew that this was just a peaceful interlude. Whatever was wrong here still existed, and these two might be angels right now, but what about tomorrow? And I *wanted* to go home.

"There's the loons," Roger said, and I saw two big birds gliding along some distance away. Their proud heads were glossy black, their backs checkered black and white, their breasts immaculate, snowy white. They were very handsome. "So that's what makes all that noise," I said.

"They're beautiful, aren't they?" Roger said. "I like to wake up in the night and hear them."

We used up an hour talking and fooling, then went swimming again. When we came out and were lying on the dock in the sun, I had definitely decided to wait out the week my mother would have wanted me to take.

I owed it to Mrs. Thornton to explain how I felt. She'd probably be relieved to have me out of the way with this mysterious crisis going on. My parents couldn't fault *that*. So I relaxed.

After we went back to the house we didn't dress, because the kids told me they wanted to go swimming again when Mac came home. We played croquet on the shady side of the house, and the grass felt good under bare feet. Mac hadn't come home by four and Tabby said, "He prob'ly stopped off to see Sharon. She's his girl."

"Oh, does he have a girl?" I was casual about it. We were sitting at the table under the maples drinking orange juice and eating cookies.

"Of course he does!" said Roger. "Aren't you somebody's girl?"

Far be it from me to admit that I was nobody's girl. So I shrugged and tried to look as if I had so many men at my feet I couldn't count them.

"We haven't seen Sharon for a long time," Tabby said sadly. "She's fun." She brightened. "Maybe she's coming home with Mac now, to go swimming!"

"Naw." Roger dismissed that. "Not unless they make up. I know they had a big fight because she never calls up here anymore and he doesn't call *her*."

"I miss her," said Tabby, rolling out her

lower lip. "When she's our sitter it's always fun."

It looked as if I was the innocent cause of trouble. Sharon and Mac were probably both dismayed by my presence, and since they couldn't fight with Mrs. Thornton they fought with each other and had broken up.

But if they really cared about each other, they should squelch their pride and make up. *I* was no threat. *I* wouldn't take him on a silver platter. If I knew how to reach her I'd tell her myself.

Walter heard the pickup coming before we did, and as it showed up over the rise he rushed to the driveway with the kids after him.

I stayed at the table sipping my drink while Mac talked to the kids. They were delighted with his news, and now I realized that some people would think he was good-looking. Not like Tom Latimer, but when he smiled it transformed his squarish face.

He went into the house and they came to me. "Mama's coming home tonight!" Tabby sang out. "She called Mac where he works!"

Mac came out in his trunks and we all went swimming again. He was moderately friendly toward me, so I challenged him to a race and he accepted, with the kids cheering from the dock. He won, and that put him in an even better mood. Maybe he *had* made up with Sharon, as well as hearing from his mother.

When we were all walking up through the pines he said mildly to me, "Any trouble with them today?"

"Nope," I said.

"Good. Because my mother's got enough on her mind without them misbehaving."

It wasn't my business to tell him that whatever he and their mother had on their minds was bothering the kids. A week from now I'd be out of the picture, never giving another thought to Hawthorne Farm.

Mac's good humor quickly wore off, and he was his old surly self when he announced it was time for him to pick up Mrs. Thornton from the airport.

"And I'm not taking you two with me," he told the kids. They started to protest but something in his tone prevented an outburst. "Mrs. Hill's coming over to sit with you. I'm taking Di."

I didn't know whether to be flattered or nervous.

I called my mother at six and told her everything was fine. Then Mrs. Hill arrived and Mac and I set out for the hour's ride in the station wagon. As we drove through the country I was mystified. Why did he want me along? If he had really made up with Sharon, maybe he wanted to tell me tactfully that I was no longer needed. That was fine with me, but what about the money? I thought that paying a sitter was a real problem with Mrs. Thornton.

Maybe Sharon was well-off and would do it out of love.

He hadn't spoken for about half an hour when he said, suddenly, "I want to talk to you before my mother gets here."

He pulled off the road to a rest area, shut off the engine, and turned in the seat to look squarely at me. "You'd better know, so my mother and I won't have to be always watching what we say in front of you."

"Mrs. Hill told me she wasn't sick." But was she? *Seriously?* I saw the kids' innocent faces, and felt that hard fist in my stomach.

"She isn't. But a lot of people are sick in the head. That's kinder than saying they're a bunch of ignorant greedy grabbers that William Thornton would disown if he was alive today! They aren't worthy of the name! Some of them aren't Thorntons by now, but they have it for middle and first names, and probably brag about their ancestor who took over a hunk of wilderness and stuck it out through the French and Indian wars."

He was fiery with pride and rage. "He held onto that land. And so did his sons and grandsons. They fought in the Revolution, and the War of 1812, and the Civil War. Hey, did you know that Hawthorne Farm was a stop on the Underground Railroad? They hid runaway slaves on the way to Canada."

He was out of breath, but only for a moment. "And in between fighting for what they thought was right, they went on helping to run the town and producing lawyers and teachers and doctors. And more good farmers, so there was always someone to carry on old William's work. Until the last Thornton to farm the place, my grandfather, was killed in World War II."

"I'm sorry," I said.

"So am I. He was my grandfather and I never got a chance to know him."

I remembered a young soldier's photograph among the others in the living room. "You look like him," I said.

Mac went on as if he hadn't heard me. "My father was the only son. Only *child*. His mother couldn't farm it alone and none of the cousins scattered over the landscape were interested. My father grew up to be a biologist, but this was where we lived even if he didn't farm it. We were *going* to, some day, when I grew up." There was a brief silence during which Mac stared straight ahead into the woods. "Well, he died," he said bluntly. "And we just kept on living on the farm, because it's home."

"Sure," I agreed. "So what's happened? Are the taxes too much?"

He groaned. "I wish it was that simple. We'd manage somehow. I'd use my college money if I had to. You know why my mother had to drop everything and go to New York? Because all the Thornton heirs are having a meeting. Most of these so-called heirs have never set foot on the place! Never gave it a thought until some hot-shot architect took it into his head to visit the home of his ancestors last summer!"

He pounded his fist on the steering wheel. "My mother already knew him and liked him; after all, he's one of the clan. He brought his kids with him, and he went around raving about how wonderful it all is, so unspoiled, and then he went away and turned the whole place into condominiums! Golf courses, tennis courts, a marina at the lake — the whole blasted works!"

It was a shocker. I said weakly, "On paper, you mean. Then what?"

"He wrote letters far and wide, called people up, and got them all interested. Or most of them. Here's this big hunk of prime real estate, including a private lake where ducks and geese come, private woods full of deer for hunting, and it belongs to *all* of them. The first Thorntons never willed off any of the property, never divided it up among their kids, because there was always somebody who wanted to stay home and farm it. If any of the kinfolk wanted to come and visit, they could. It would have gone along like this forever until this — this —" he couldn't think of a word bad enough. "This *spoiler* sneaked in, and all he could see were the dollar signs. So they're going to form a corporation. Hawthorne Estates, Incorporated," he said viciously.

"But what about *your* family? Will you be

evicted from your own house? How can they do that?"

"They can't evict us off the property, because we're heirs, too. But it's not our house, though it's the only home my father ever knew, and the same with us. It belongs to the estate and we even have to pay rent. But it's small, because we're caretakers, you might say. We can't afford to live in another place that would be halfway decent. An apartment somewhere, or a house squeezed up in town — we'd all go crazy!"

He beat his fist on the wheel again. "I wish that — *spoiler* had had a fatal accident on the way here that day. No, I guess I don't wish that on anyone. My father died in an accident, and this jerk has a couple of kids. But *they'd* have plenty to live on, whereas we have just what my mother makes teaching, and what I can earn. Only, we always thought we were rich because of the farm, and now they want to take it away from us."

"If they can't throw you out, why can't you go on living in the house?"

"Oh, that will come down. That's where the clubhouse will be. I've seen the first sketches. See, we can have one of those blasted condominiums for our share of the big bucks that'll be rolling in." He laughed harshly. "Can you imagine living there like *that*, knowing how it all used to be? A golf course where the old orchard is? Big outboards and water skiers destroying the loons' and the grebes' habitat? *We* let people use the lake, but no outboards."

If they weren't going to be thrown out, a nice modern condominium would be a fair exchange, I thought. *Imagine all that life and fun going on, transforming the wilderness!* He was too young to be so set in his ways. His crazy, laughing loons could move somewhere else, there must be other lakes. I didn't even know what a grebe was.

"So you don't have to think of being crammed into an apartment or a house in town," I began. "Even if things were changed you'd still be home — in a way," I added feebly.

He turned and glared at me through the dusk. "Sure! Home where they bring in the bulldozers! Great unspoiled country, fellers, so let's get in there and spoil it! That tree'll have to go, and *that* one. Who cares if you wipe out seventy-five years in five minutes with a chain saw? And brother, can we blast those geese when they come down to feed and rest in the fall!"

There was nothing I could say to this passionate outburst.

"Thanks for listening to me," Mac said gruffly. "I can't sound off like this to my mother. She's got enough on her mind."

"I'm glad to be useful," I said weakly. "You mentioned your college money. What are you going to be?"

"I *was* going to agricultural college," he said. "I *was* going to farm the place."

"Maybe you can farm part of it," I suggested. "You'd have a ready market for everything you raised, and milk and eggs and stuff."

That did not deserve an answer, apparently. He started up the engine and we drove the rest of the way in silence. I was really sorry he and the family felt so bad, but they'd get over it. I'd never say so, because I hate being told that when I'm sunk in the depths. But, personally, I thought it all sounded good. It was progress. Nothing stands still, life goes on and you have to go with it. In this case the finished product would be worth all the trouble and work, and there'd still be plenty of fresh air, and some of the woods left, and the lake. But it would be different.

$\mathcal{S}even$

Soon we were driving into the city, surrounded by its brilliant lights and the hum and go of it. I loved the excitement of the big airport. If only Mac hadn't been so depressed. I told myself that a year from now he'd be pretty cheerful about it all, even if he couldn't believe it now.

When Mac went to meet his mother he was smiling as if everything was fine, and he did have a nice smile, though he certainly didn't waste it on just anybody. He hugged and kissed her without embarrassment, then nodded at me.

"I brought Di," he said.

She gave me a warm smile and a handshake. She was a slim, dark, attractive woman; Roger resembled her, but I could see a bit of Tabby, too.

"Diana, you look like your mother. Or do you hate hearing that?"

"Nope. I'm proud of it."

"Good for you." She took my arm and Mac's so we could walk three abreast. "How are you getting along with the children?"

"We're still circling each other like strange dogs, but today there were a few wags."

I liked her laugh. I liked *her*, period. She was one of those persons with whom rapport is instant. And Mac had become a different boy from the moment he first saw her in the crowd. I kept wanting to look at him again to see if that nice stranger was still there. But I felt suddenly clumsy, as if that nice stranger had knocked me off balance; as if he'd been there all the time, but in disguise.

I got into the second seat, and nothing important was said until we were out of the airport traffic and on the highway heading into the countryside.

"I filled Di in on everything," he said. "I thought it was better all around."

"So she won't think she's walked into a Gothic novel where everybody's concealing an evil secret?" She looked around at me.

"Yup, like which room has the monster in it," I said.

"It would have to be the room behind Roger's," she said. "We really must see if something's living among all those trunks. We may be harboring a whole colony of Thornton ghosts."

"They're probably leaving in droves," said Mac dismally. "Getting out before the roof falls in. Gone back to spin in their graves."

I sat forward. "The evil secret is that with all this going on I'm just an embarrassment around here. I mean, when you worked this up with my mother you didn't know this other thing was going to happen so fast."

"I didn't expect *dear* cousin Miles to move so soon," she said dryly, "but he's been quite the busy little bee, getting everyone rounded up."

"Well, here I am, a stranger, and you sure don't need me when you've got so much on your mind. The kids were talking about some sitter they liked." I looked at the back of Mac's head, but he could have been a robot chauffeur.

"Oh, my dear," said his mother, "you're not a stranger! You're Cora's girl. Even your voice is familiar to me! I'm really looking forward to working with you, and if you're as good with children as your mother claims, you're necessary to us."

"But with all this *upheaval* —"

"It's all an emotional upheaval right now. The physical part, with the bulldozers and the chainsaws, won't be starting yet."

"Then it's a sure thing?" Mac said tightly.

"The loan is. So they'll be drafting the papers now for the final approval. Our little handful stood out against it, but we were swamped." Now she sounded weary as she named names that Mac knew. A great-uncle; some distant cousins who had known and loved the farm in their youth; a Californian branch that had made the pilgrimage a year ago to discover their roots, and hoped to come again; and a few younger relatives who were against developments anywhere except to improve slum housing.

"Otherwise, of all William Thornton's descendants who were able to show up, or give their proxies, the majority is for Hawthorne Estates, Incorporated. Of course there'll be another vote to approve the final plans, but that's just a technicality."

"How long do we have in the house before they knock it down for their clubhouse and bar?"

"Blessings on the red tape, dear. There have to be soil tests done to see if the place will support the enormous septic system necessary. The water situation must be checked out. All kinds of permits granted. Your Great Uncle Matthew took me out for a cup of tea and said they were hoping to find some endangered species somewhere on the place. As if they haven't already been everywhere on the property, bird-watching and botanizing." She laughed sadly. "He was so darned brave and hopeful when we'd just been hearing Miles' ideas for the other side of the lake."

"You mean the Forest Primeval?" Mac spoke with difficulty.

"I'm afraid so. Unless Matthew's endangered species turns out to be a surviving dinosaur."

"All we've got," Mac said, "is something

perfect. So of course it has to be destroyed as soon as possible."

"Mac, Mac," his mother said softly. "It's not going to happen tomorrow."

"But it *is* going to happen," he protested. "It'll all be wiped out as if a war ran over it. With that bunch of relatives, who's afraid of the Mafia?"

I had a queasy feeling that his eyes were full of tears. I could hear them in his voice, and something in me turned over. I wanted to put my hands on his shoulders and give him a warm squeeze, but I didn't know him that well. He was probably hating me this instant for hearing his outburst. So I sank back and tried to pretend I wasn't there.

In a little while he said calmly, "Sorry for that. There'll be no more of it, I promise you."

"We have a right to be angry," his mother said, "and to express it. As long as it doesn't become an obsession that warps our lives. We're all going to survive this thing, you know."

Mac didn't answer.

When we arrived at the house the children were in bed, and Mrs. Hill had the teakettle on.

She and Mrs. Thornton talked about the house and the kids and the latest doings among the neighbors. Mac ate and drank in sullen silence, until Mrs. Hill said to him, "Your friends have been scratching at the back door. I told 'em they'd have to wait for you. You're the soft touch around here."

Mac's face changed instantly, lighting up in that all-too-rare smile. He left the table and took a paper bag from one end of the bench where the cats were also having a snack. Walter got up, but Mac said, "Stay," and went out.

"What is it?" I asked Mrs. Thornton.

"Go out and see. But be quiet. Don't make any sudden moves, or speak. Your voice will be strange to them."

I opened the door without a sound. Mac was sitting on the porch steps, and he was talking to something I couldn't see at first, in the affectionate voice I'd heard last night. Then, in the light from the kitchen windows, I saw the first raccoons I'd ever seen away from greeting cards or place mats. Real, living raccoons, with small, velvety, stand-up ears, and adorable little faces with black masks across eyes which sparkled like dark gems as they caught the light; tiny black hands reached for the cookies Mac handed out. Each animal took its cookie and sat down to eat it, holding the cookie in both hands and nibbling away, chewing very thoroughly. They had beautiful fur coats and thick tails ringed round and round with black.

I stood there holding my breath, trying to see everything at once. "Come on, Little Sister, come on," Mac coaxed softly, and one came forward who looked almost silver, and her mask could have been black satin. She had a hard time making up her mind to take the cookie, though she wanted it so much. Finally she took it.

I didn't dare shift a foot, I was so afraid of breaking up the meeting. At last one of them ran off, and the rest followed. I let my breath out, and without looking around Mac said gruffly, "Thanks for being so quiet."

"I was spellbound. They're so darling and so beautiful. Why did they go like that?"

"Some of them have babies, and sometimes I figure they're saying to themselves, 'Gosh, I'd better get back home and see what those kids are up to.' "

We both laughed. "Do you ever see the babies?" I asked.

"Oh, sure. They'll start bringing them some night."

"How can you tell them apart?"

"They all look different when you know them. One of them, Sophie, must be everybody's grandmother by now. All I know is, when *she* shows up everybody moves out of the way." He sounded easy and relaxed.

"What happens to them if — well, you know?" I was surprised at how anxious I felt.

"They'll do all right. Raccoons always manage as long as nobody's trapping or shooting them." I winced. "But Sophie now, she's getting gray. She's an old girl now, and she knows our voices as well as we know her. The people who'll be here won't give a hoot, they'll just think the raccoons are pests to be gotten rid of."

"If you stayed on here even in a condominium, you could look out for Sophie, couldn't you?"

He didn't answer that. In the black night silence that pressed down upon us, there was an odd, abrupt, echoing cough from beyond the barn, then the sound of something running, and then silence again.

"What's *that*?" I gasped, ready to clutch him as I waited for It to sneak up on us. The night turned even blacker.

"It's a deer. More than one. That cough is a warning, and now they've gone."

"What frightened them?" I asked nervously, staring all about me. Fireflies winked off and on against the darkness, and the honeysuckle surrounded us with a fragrance it never had during the day.

"It could be anything. Don't worry, nothing's after us," he said contemptuously. "The monsters are all somewhere else, getting ready to attack."

The warm, caring Mac had gone with the raccoons and the deer. As if to finish off the moment, the loons started their weird duet out on the lake.

E^{ight}

The next morning I woke up early, with the rooster crowing, and the barn swallows chattering and swooping and soaring like mad.

I heard the pickup drive out, and I remembered Mac's voice last night when he talked about the fate of Hawthorne Farm. I remembered how, when he had met his mother, he had seemed so confident and mature. And then later, after an outburst in the car, he had apologized without awkwardness. He'd been a man, not a teenager. Then still another Mac fed the raccoons, loving them and being trusted by them.

How many Macs had I met since I got off the bus in town? And I'd thought he was just dogged, dull, and disgusted with everything, mostly me.

As I took my turn in the bathroom before the kids were stirring, I realized I hadn't thought of Tom Latimer since I put on my swimsuit yesterday afternoon. I also realized that I wasn't planning on going home in a week, much as I wanted to. Mrs. Thornton had told me I was necessary, darn it!

My lessons started at seven-thirty sharp, with two ten-minute breaks. The kids cleared up the breakfast dishes, tidied their rooms, tended the hens, and gathered the eggs. They filled the bird baths and they also had to put in a short stint weeding the vegetable garden.

I'd never worked alone with a teacher before and felt self-conscious at first, but Mrs. Thornton was business-like and yet friendly. We started off by reviewing, so she could find out where I began to fall back in math and Latin. She asked me if I disliked reading, and I said I loved to read, but somehow I hadn't done much in the last few months. However, I'd already started on my list. We decided that I was to read a certain amount before tomorrow, then we'd discuss what I'd read. Because she considered reading so important, the kids had a half-hour reading every morning, after their chores, and a quiet hour after lunch. I could do much of my own reading then. I didn't have to stare at the kids every moment, just as long as I didn't forget them when they were out of sight. They should come when I rang the bell that stood on the kitchen mantel.

I had telephone numbers for her at the college and for Mac at work, along with those for the police, the fire department, and the family doctor.

At ten-thirty the kids and Walter rode off in the station wagon with Mrs. Thornton as far as the road, so I was actually *alone* for a few minutes. Though I'd been in old houses before, because of my mother's work, I'd never been in one that stood all by itself in what was virtually a foreign country. Once the sound of the station wagon died away I could hear those ticks and creaks.

It's talking about me, I thought. *It knows I'm an outsider. It doesn't like me because I don't think condominiums are so bad.*

What if I heard the latch lift in the room at the head of the stairs? I was just about to leap for the door and rush outside to the birds when the telephone rang.

I was standing right beside it in the front hall, and I nearly went through the ceiling. Then I grabbed it.

"H-hello?" I said nervously. If nobody had answered, I wouldn't have been surprised.

There was a short silence, then a girl's voice said, "Is this the Thornton residence?" She sounded uncertain, which made me feel better.

"Yes, it is," I answered.

"Who is *this*?" A little sharp now.

"I'm the sitter, Diana Moore. Who are *you*?"

"Is Mac there?"

"No, he's at work. Would you like to leave a message?"

"Where is he working?"

What manners! "All I know is that he's painting a house." The telephone number was for an emergency, and I didn't consider this an emergency.

She hung up. *Slammed* up is more like it.

"It was nice talking to you, too," I said. "We must do it again sometime." Now I had something else to think about. Was that Sharon? Knowing what it was like to be crazy about a boy, I could be sympathetic. Probably Mac could be very attractive at times. I'd had glimpses of it. But she might have been a little more polite.

I went outside and sat on the porch. A few minutes later, Roger and Tabby joined me. I decided to try to glean a little information from them.

"A girl just called up and asked for Mac," I said, nonchalantly.

"Sharon," they said almost together.

"How do you know? There could be lots of girls calling Mac."

"Uh-uh." Tabby tucked in her lips and shook her head.

"Mac doesn't like girls now," Roger said with satisfaction.

I wondered what Sharon was like. I saw her as petite and blonde, riding a bicycle all over the village today, searching for Mac painting a house.

Maybe they'd make up and then he wouldn't be around in his spare time. Not that he was much company for me, but I felt a chill of loneliness. Tom sparkled in my gloom like the Impossible Dream.

It was useless to tell myself it was my own fault, for goofing off in school. Useless to tell myself I didn't want Mac, I wanted Tom Latimer. Here I was in exile, and I'd just begun thinking Mac could make it bearable, and *now* —

I sighed deeply, and then realized both kids were staring at me.

"Well!" I said briskly. "What do we do till lunch? Is there anything you haven't shown me?"

"The hill where we go coasting," said Tabby.

"The old cemetery," said Roger. "It's on the way to Strawberry Hill."

It sounded pretty grim, but it wasn't on that bright summer day, with wild flowers growing around the old stones in the little clearing. Leaves rustled softly, and robins sang loud and cheerfully. The kids casually named names as if they personally knew all those long-ago people, and visited them often.

By the time we'd climbed Strawberry Hill, stood on a stone wall and looked over a dip in the trees to a white church steeple in the distance, picked and ate handfuls of wild strawberries, watched ravens flying over, (my first live ones, ever) we'd used up the morning. I wondered how Sharon was doing.

Back at the house, we once more assembled our lunches. The kitchen looked like a disaster area, and we cleaned it up before we took our provisions down to the lake, attended of course by Walter and the cats. I ignored the dark menace of the Forest Primeval over there until Roger announced that he was going to live there when he grew up.

Choice residential sites, lake frontage. That's what the Forest Primeval would be as soon as the red tape was untangled. I looked away from Roger's radiant face. Then Tabby said she planned to live out in the orchard some day.

Private golf course overlooking crystal lake. That was the future of the orchard.

I was angry. Somebody should be preparing these kids for what was going to happen! To get the news all at once could be traumatic. I wouldn't dare tell Mrs. Thornton that, I thought, but I'd tell Mac, if I ever had a chance to get him alone now that he and Sharon had probably had their grand reunion.

"What if you get married and your husband doesn't like it out here in the country?" I asked Tabby. "What if he thinks it's too wild and lonely?"

"It isn't wild and lonely. It's *home*. And if people don't like it, I just won't marry them," Tabby said grandly.

This place might not be my idea of paradise, but it was heaven for these two. I was definitely depressed. Whether it was because of the kids, or Sharon, or both, I didn't know. But it was there, all right.

"Quiet hour!" I announced. We'd brought our books: *The Borrowers* for Tabby, *Treasure Island* for Roger, and I was back with *A Tale of Two Cities*.

I needed some time to think, there were so many new ideas floating around in my head. I was still jumpy about where I was; I mean, all this solitude and space makes you feel so *infinitesimal*.

The three of us sat quietly thinking and reading for a long while. Suddenly Roger sat up.

"Mac's home!" he yelled. I could hear the pickup roaring faintly. The kids went whooping toward the house, making the woods echo. I went slowly, carrying the tote bag, bracing myself for the smiles of a happy boy. At least medium-happy. Even with all the worries about the farm he'd still be more cheerful if he and his girl had made up. And if I couldn't have my chance with Tom Latimer, it was pretty tough to be forced to watch other people being in love.

He was already in the house changing when I got there, and when we met to go swimming he looked just the same as usual. Preoccupied, but not with rapture. Maybe Sharon hadn't found him. Should I tell him she'd called? But then, how did I know it was Sharon? If the kids told him, so be it.

"How are things?" he asked me.

"Great," I said.

We had a good time in the lake. He helped the kids work on their swimming; he was an awfully nice big brother even if he didn't like *me*. The kids wanted us to race again and we did, with them cheering us impartially from the dock, and Walter barking in joyous excitement. The race was a tie. Mac acted liberated and happy in the water, and I felt different myself. But he went back to the usual glum mood while we were drying ourselves off and walking back to the house.

Mrs. Thornton was home. She had changed into a swimsuit, with a light robe over it, and dinner had been started. She looked pretty and surprisingly young.

"I'll take a quiet dip before we eat," she said.

"We'll go with you," Roger announced, but she smiled and shook her head.

"Not this time, love, I need to be alone to collect my thoughts."

"Anything new?" Mac asked.

"Nothing. Don't worry. It was awfully hot and noisy today, that's all. Everybody get dressed, and after dinner we'll have a good hard game of croquet."

"Oh boy!" Tabby exclaimed.

"Be careful!" Mac shouted after her. He had that grim look again. I got quickly out of the way before I could see in his face the regret that he'd told me anything.

N^{ine}

During dinner and three out-for-blood croquet games, you'd never dream anything was
wrong. I knew it was all for Roger's and
Tabby's sakes, but I still thought it was
wrong not to start preparing them for the
changes. Mac and his mother weren't able to
look on the positive side, except to be positive
it was all going to be terrible, but they'd
better think up something good about it
pretty soon and pass it on to Roger and
Tabby. Those kids were really going to suffer
unless they learned about the development in
easy stages.

If I ever got Mac alone, I'd tell him. Those
green eyes would freeze me and I'd be told to
mind my own business, but I didn't care. If I
was the sitter, the kids *were* my business.

While throwing myself into the games as if
I had a killer instinct, I listened for the tele-

phone to ring. But Sharon didn't call, and Mac didn't call *her*. At dusk, when the fireflies were beginning to twinkle around us, the kids went up to bed and their mother followed to read to them. Mac said abruptly to me, "Want to go out on the lake?"

"Sure," I said. I couldn't be positive his mother hadn't suggested it, but there we were, out in the rowboat because I wasn't used to canoes. "We'll try that in broad daylight," he said.

He rowed straight out to the middle of the lake, gently dipping the oars. They made little silver whirlpools in the quiet water. The lake was a broad, pale glimmer under the last light in the sky, but the surrounding woods looked black and deadly. We were heading for the Forest Primeval, and even to *think* those words gave me chills.

He stopped rowing, and we drifted. The first stars were out and reflecting in the lake, and the Forest Primeval loomed higher and higher above us. I thought I could see the shore.

We headed back across the lake in a roundabout way. I wasn't so nervous about it now that we were leaving.

"What are you going to be?" he asked me, as if making polite conversation. "Do you know yet?"

"I'm going to art school," I said. "I plan to design clothes to order." I added casually, "Already I do most of my own, and some for other people, too."

"That sounds like a good business." He was still polite, but that was all.

We landed and he tied up the boat. Once we left the beach for the pines, it was very dark, and we hadn't brought a flashlight. I tripped over something — my own feet, probably — and he took a firm hold of my elbow and shoved me along until we came out into the open. The lighted windows of the house were rosy-gold against the dark.

"For over three hundred years lights have been in that house," he said in a low voice. "First it was candles. They must have been pretty dim, and scarce, because you couldn't waste them. Then it was oil lamps. Now, after these lamps are put out — *nothing*. After three hundred years."

Without planning it I put my hand on his arm and squeezed it. "Mac, I'm so sorry," I said.

"Thanks, Di," he muttered. And he put his hand over mine and gave it a quick, hard squeeze back. Our hands held for a moment, then separated as Walter came to meet us. He led the way to the house, where Mrs. Thornton was clearing school papers off the kitchen table.

"Cocoa, you two?" she asked cheerfully.

My little room looked good to me that night. I didn't even mind the night noises, or lack of them. Full of good resolutions, I worked on my Latin for almost an hour after I got into bed. In the back of my mind I was remembering what Mac said about candles three hundred years ago, and I wondered how many girls had slept in this room, maybe writing in their diaries by candlelight, or composing love letters by lamplight. Or reading romantic poetry (which I'd have done if there'd been any handy) and then lying in the dark looking forward to tomorrow.

Because that's what I was doing.

My lessons went well after that first week, and we had perfect weather. The kids and I ate out every noon, down at the lake, or in the tree house, or out on Magic Mountain, or under Robin Hood's Oak.

Then Mac would arrive and we'd all go swimming, and sometimes we were still there when Mrs. Thornton came home. After supper there had to be croquet, or a softball game including five people and Walter, who was better than anyone else at catching the ball and running with it, so a lot of time was spent running after Walter.

Then Mac and I went out on the lake during the sunset, and I learned to row and to fish. He was always matter-of-fact, but sometimes when we were walking home afterwards, our hands came together, and we walked that way almost to the house.

On my first weekend, the weather was still good. On Saturday Mrs. Thornton took the kids into town while she shopped for groceries, and Mac gave me my first canoeing lesson. The sun was misty and the lake was silver instead of blue, except in the dark green shade of the woods. Canoeing was marvelous. We went all the way across to the Forest Primeval. The loons called, and we saw ducks and heard them softly quacking.

"The Forest Primeval doesn't look half bad," I said. "Someday I might even have the courage to walk into it. For about six feet."

He laughed. "Oh, it's nice in there. Lots of sun gets through."

Two people were sliding a canoe off the sandy shore under the giant trees. They waved, and Mac waved back.

"Where did *they* come from?" I asked.

"There's an old trail coming through from the highway. They carried the canoe in. I told you, we let people use it. Canoers like it because nobody's racing by making big waves, the same big waves that swamp nests."

I still liked the idea of the lake all alive with bright-colored boats racing by, and handsome boys and girls on water skis. But at the same time I was loving it at this moment, with the canoe gliding above its shimmering reflection. For me there were two different lakes. Like the two (or more) different Macs.

"Well, I'd like to play all day," he said finally, "but them days is gone forever, as the old feller says."

"What old feller?"

"Old MacLeod Thornton, that's who," he wheezed. He was actually joking, and *I* was responsible. I felt proud. "He's got to stir his ancient bones," Mac went on, "and mow a few miles of grass."

"It's my duty to help the gentleman," I said. "If I can't assist him across a busy street, like the good Girl Scout that I am, I can mow. I do at home."

"You're on!"

The canoe slipped across the lustrous water toward the pines. I was feeling happy, which was as much of a surprise as Mac's joking. We pulled the canoe up together and turned it over, and walked up through the pines. I was ahead, and just as we came out into the open, Mac put his hands on either side of my waist and turned me toward him. Was he going to kiss me? If he did would I know if this whole mixed-up summer had been meant to be?

He was looking solemnly into my eyes — that unmistakable look — and I was holding my breath. Then his eyes shifted, he glanced past my shoulder, and his eyes narrowed. His hands bit into my sides and then let go. "What are *they* doing here?" His voice was soft with rage.

Ten

There was a black and silver sports car parked up by the house, and two tall, very blond people were standing near it. Walter was being extremely hospitable.

"The boy's making notes," I said resentfully, "and *she's* got a camera, and she's pointing at the big maples. Who are they?"

"Thorntons, though I hate to admit it," Mac said in disgust. "Look at Walter! Standing there wagging his tail, the big idiot."

"He must know they're relatives."

"Relatives! That man is even named for one of old William's sons, Joshua, and he's figuring out how to bulldoze the place to the ground. *She's* probably talking about sawing down the maples. Daddy's little helpers in the Search and Destroy Mission."

He whistled sharply, and Walter raced down to meet us. "You shouldn't have let them step out of the car, you traitor," Mac said sternly. He was very pale. The blonds were strolling toward us. "Hot-Shot Junior and the Crown Princess," said Mac.

The two could have been a couple of high-priced models who had walked straight out of a glossy magazine. They were both tanned darker than their hair. Hers was artfully tousled and shoulder-length, his cut short but loose and soft, the kind you'd like to run your fingers through. I mean, *some* girls would.

"Hi, Mac!" he called, taking off his sunglasses. She pushed hers up on her head. (Mine never stay, but mine are cheap.) "Hello, Mac," she said. Mac didn't answer.

Joshua could have been designed for his off-white corduroy jeans and pastel-plaid sportshirt, they looked so great on him. Right away I detested his sister for being one of these lanky, hipless girls who'd look good in something run up out of an old bedspread. She was wearing blue sailcloth slacks and a voluminous top in big blue and white checks, cinched in with a rope belt around her incredibly narrow waist. It was something I'd be scared to try even if I could afford such expensive clothes.

"We're June and Josh Thornton," she said to me, smiling graciously. "And you're . . . ?"

"Diana Moore," I said.

Josh said lazily, "Nice to meet you, Diana Moore." And then I saw his eyes. Had I thought Tom Latimer's were the bluest? I was wrong. Josh Thornton's were intense blue, almost turquoise, set under eyebrows like golden wings.

Mac said harshly, "What do you want here? Got a fleet of dozers stashed around the bend?"

"Keep your cool, man." Josh wasn't upset. "We're spending some time at Elliot Thornton's, and we just dropped in to take a look around."

"After all, we have a right," his sister said pleasantly. I knew I was right to detest her. "We're just getting some preliminary notes together. It will be quite marvelous to turn this wasteland into something beautiful."

"Yeah, like one big parking lot," said Mac. He strode past them toward the barn, snapping his fingers for Walter to go with him. I followed loyally, and the golden pair kept up with me.

"That barn's really *built*," Josh said. "Fascinating construction. Shame it can't be incorporated into the complex somehow. But it's where we want to build the first unit. There'll be a tremendous view of the lake once we clear out most of those pines."

I looked back at the pines and thought of the breeze stirring through them, their good smell, and the way they looked against sunny skies or starry ones. I looked up at the barn, and even though I was all for the project I thought of the barn swallows coming next spring and finding their home gone. There'd been as many generations of swallows living in that barn as the years since it had been built. What would they *do*? They'd be frantic!

If only there were a way to prepare them, as the children should be prepared. It was so grim, I had to hastily divert my thoughts.

The other two had been happily rambling on, and now I heard June say, "Those two old maples will have to come down. If there's a decent cellar under the house that'll be a good start on the excavation for the heated pool."

The lawn mower roared into life behind the barn, and I ran out there. Mac didn't want my help. He ignored me when I shouted at him over the noise, and his face was set like pale stone. Our hours on the lake this morning, our quiet talk and our mild joking, the moment when I'd expected our first kiss — they were all gone as if they'd never been. Those other two Thorntons with their turquoise eyes had done it. I hated them.

I detoured so I wouldn't have to face them again, and went into the house and called home. I told my mother I was still getting along fine. "If you're alone in the house, tell me what Madge's son is like," she said. "I hope he's being nice to you and you're having some fun. He has a girl, I suppose, but he must have introduced you to other people your own age."

"He's nice, Mother, and yes, I've already met some other kids." It was a white lie. I'd talked to an anonymous girl on the telephone, and as for those two now strolling in the orchard, probably planning out the golf course, could you call them kids in the usual sense? They acted so sophisticated and rich and powerful.

"Di?" my mother said.

"I was just looking out the window," I said. "Some kind of odd birds in the orchard."

"*You're* interested in identifying birds?" She sounded amused.

"Don't knock it, Mummie dear. It's one of the most exciting activities around here. Even the little kids are experts."

"Di, are you really all right?"

"I really am, Mother. I'm going ahead like anything in my work. Mrs. Thornton is nice and she makes everything so clear and interesting. Mac and I were canoeing on the lake this morning, and we only came in because he has to mow. I'm going to help him now."

I did try again, but he ignored me. He was so pale his hair looked ink-black and his eyes green as the new-cut grass. I knew that every time he got a glimpse of those two he must have been sick with rage. I was helpless; I couldn't do a thing about it.

I went back into the house and brought my math book down to the kitchen. At least I could get something done on my weekend assignment. Then Josh walked in without knocking and got a drink of water. Lounging against the sink, he said, "Where do you fit in around here, Di?"

I had a feeling that he was on a hunting

expedition. Like Tom Latimer, he couldn't resist using his charm on the nearest female. I'd have enjoyed Tom's efforts; I'd have tried to charm him back. But Josh Thornton was harassing Mac, and that turned me against him from the start.

"Cat got your tongue?" he asked.

"I'm just awe-struck. Do you often make these sudden visits to the peasants?"

He laughed. "Gosh, I thought I'd fool folks in this here frog disguise. Yes, Di, I've been looking for the right girl to kiss me and turn me back into a prince."

"I wouldn't take a chance if I was invited," I said. "Not being royalty myself, *I* might turn into a frog, too." I flipped a page and stared hard at figures that made no sense to me whatever.

He came and leaned over my shoulder. "What are you doing? Oh. That's a piece of cake. You must have had real trouble with math, if you're doing summer work. Of course there's a theory that male brains have a different construction than females', that's why we're so good at math and most girls aren't."

"I don't believe that," I said haughtily. "I happen to be very good at anything that interests me. Math never did, that's all."

"You see? It's because of that difference in the brain cells."

"I know some girls who are crazy about calculus and trigonometry and stuff like that."

"Oh, there are a few rare exceptions. Occasionally a girl can think like a man. Like my sister. She's studying to be an architect, and so am I."

"Oh? The way you two talked about taking down trees I thought you were training to be lumberjacks."

He laughed. "Touché. But you can't make an omelet without breaking eggs, and I think the old Thorntons would be pretty proud at what some of their descendants can accomplish." He looked around him. "When old William built that fireplace and hewed out those beams, he never dreamed that —"

"Some day it would all be replaced by a swimming pool," I said sweetly.

"You don't approve of a swimming pool, Princess Di?"

"Not when a real treasure like a perfectly sound 17th-century house is destroyed to make room for it."

I saw the change in his eyes and a whitening around his nostrils. I knew I had angered him, and I was glad.

"And now if you'll excuse me, I have work to do with my feeble female brain."

The mower had stopped, and Mac came across the porch. He held the screen door open. "Outside, Thornton," he said. "You may have a right to prowl and pry outside, but while my family is paying rent, this is our house, so get out."

"Relax, Mac, I'm leaving." Josh sauntered

out past him. June was standing by the steps. "We'll be back."

"Don't be in too much of a rush," Mac said. "The so-called corporation hasn't gotten off the ground yet. You've just begun applying for all the permits you'll need."

"But we know the right people, Mac," said June silkily. "We're in the majority, and we have the clout, dear cousin. You and your mother had better climb onto the bandwagon. You owe it to yourselves and your little brother and sister." She smiled at me past his rigid shoulder. "Nice meeting you, Di."

"Yes, it was," Josh drawled. "Good luck with your math. Maybe the Great Stone Face here can help you out."

The privileged two went to the black and silver car and Josh slid behind the wheel. They buckled up and put on their sunglasses, the engine roared, then the car circled and sped out. As it went out of sight, the horn sounded insolently.

Mac stood like a statue until the car disappeared. Then he sagged back against a porch post, shaking his head. I wanted to do something, but I didn't know what, so I put my hand timidly on his shoulder.

He jumped as if I'd stabbed him. "Mac, they're *awful*," I said.

He ground one fist into the other palm, and didn't speak. It was as if he didn't trust himself even to try. Then he walked away toward the mower, got it going, and went off out of sight behind the woodshed.

I stood in the driveway and looked at the house. It lay there like an old gray dog peacefully drowsing in the sun. As Walter would be when he got old, but still faithful and loving. Yes, *loving*. Maybe that was a crazy word for a house, but I felt it then. It had sheltered people ever since William Thornton had built that first cabin, which was now the kitchen. It had protected them through Indian attacks and blizzards and wars. Thorntons were born under its roof, and stayed, or went out into the world. They died and more were born, and the house was always there: patient, protective, welcoming.

But *those* two had the nerve to stroll in here looking like pretty paper dolls, and talk as if it were so much junk to be demolished by a wave of the hand. I actually growled, and did the same thing with my fist that Mac had done with his.

Mac could use up some of his rage pushing the heavy mower. I touched my toes thirty times, turned some cartwheels, and then shadow-boxed all the way back to the house. First my target was Josh, then it was June, then Josh again. So girls lacked the necessary brain cells, did they?

I completed the assignment with no trouble at all. It must have been all the adrenalin coursing through my system. I didn't even realize the mower had stopped until Mac was coming in the door. He'd taken off his shirt long before, and his brown skin was wet and shiny with sweat. He had a long drink of water, and then he said gruffly, "I'm going for a swim. You coming?"

"Sure!" I ran up to my room by the twisting back stairs, feeling a genuine affection for them. I've always been for the underdog, and now the house was the underdog. I put on my suit with no vain glance in the mirror this time, grabbed a beach towel, and ran down again.

I was still mad when I hit the water. Now I understood with my heart, not just with my brain, what Mac and his mother were feeling, and I shared their helpless anger. Loving, caring, being fiercely protective — none of it was any good if you didn't have the power to back it up. *The clout*, as the unspeakable June had elegantly put it.

I hated *her*, I hated her brother. Those two had violently changed my life in one hour. I forged ahead in the lake like an Olympic competitor.

"Hey!" Mac caught up with me. "Head back in!"

"Okay!" I tread water. "You want any mountains moved? I've got all this energy because I'm so furious."

"What about? Geometry?"

"No! *Them*! The Jays! Josh and June, the Jerks!"

He grinned for the first time in hours. "I've got dirtier names than that, but I'll keep 'em to myself. Come on, head back in."

We raced for the shore, and Walter splashed out to meet us. Inkie and Snow sat on the dock. When we were wading in Mac said, "If being furious could do it, I'd have shifted a lot of people into outer space by now."

We rubbed our hair and dried our ears. The pine fragrance was strong in the still air. Out on the lake the loons began calling, and a pair of handsome ducks came in quite near. "Listen," Mac said, "don't say anything to my mother about those two. I mean, no sense fouling up the weekend."

"I won't say anything. But who's Elliot Thornton?"

He laughed scornfully. "A third cousin. His branch struck it rich on Wall Street, so he's what you call a gentleman farmer. Somebody else does all the work. He never pitched hay or plowed a field in his life. Always talking about his forefathers settling this part of the country. He has a big house, keeps horses and pedigreed cattle, but he can't wait to turn the old Thornton homestead into big bucks."

"Does he ever come around here?"

"I don't think he has the nerve to face us. Oh, he'll show up when all this is wiped out. Just multiply the Jerks by thirty or more, and you can see what chance any of *us* has." I knew his *us* included the life on and around the lake, in the woods, and the woods themselves. Now my indignation even took in the Forest Primeval over there; it was no longer menacing, but as innocent and helpless as the house.

Mac, walking ahead of me through the pines, looked defeated. Without thinking first I grabbed his arm with both hands. "Oh, Mac, there should be *something* we could do!"

Mac stared at me as if he'd never seen me before. Then very gently he took me by the shoulders and very gently kissed me. I kissed him back, and then we hugged each other and just sort of clung with all our strength. It was weird, but wonderful, too. I remember Walter gazing up at us, tail slowly waving. Inkie chased Snow up a tree. And Mac and I still hugged.

Then Walter grumbled in his throat, and stared up the path. Somehow we separated but each kept an arm about the other. We were standing there like Siamese twins when this girl appeared in the opening. She stared at us with huge dark eyes, and she was absolutely white with shock.

I knew who it had to be before Mac said quietly, "Hi, Sharon."

She was slight, with short and very shiny dark brown hair, and in her shorts and sleeveless top she didn't look any bigger than Roger.

"Who does she sit for?" she asked huskily. I recognized the voice. "The little ones or you? She's pretty darned efficient, isn't she?"

"Now, wait a minute, Sharon," Mac began, but she spun away and ran. I've been in that position myself at least once, enough to know just what a stab to the heart it could be. I felt guilty, but resentful, too, because *my* moment had been spoiled.

"You'd better go talk to her, Mac," I said.

"What would I say? We've broken up, and she was ready for it."

"Looks as if she's changed her mind."

"Well, I haven't changed mine." He kissed me again, this time not so gently. So I decided to forget the guilt and enjoy myself. I heard her car driving away and thought, *Sorry, Sharon, I really am.*

She must have passed Mrs. Thornton on the way out, because the station wagon came in as we reached the house. There were two extra children, brought along to spend the afternoon with Roger and Tabby, so after lunch Mac and I took a long walk. In the woods we visited another cabin site, where the ruins of an old chimney still remained. A clear brown brook bubbled along nearby, and we sat down beside it while he told me who used to live here. Another Thornton, of course.

"Roger wants a log cabin in the Forest Primeval," I said. "Mac, those kids ought to be told."

"*No!* Not until the last gun's fired, and we have to strike our colors. Because, even if I know it's useless, I keep on hoping for miracles."

"Well, miracles have happened," I said.

"How many can you personally count?" He was cynical.

"Apart from the ones in the Bible, what

about the times in history when all was lost and then was suddenly saved? The wind changing in time to turn back a terrible fire? Rain coming in time to end a drought that would have meant famine? People cast upon a desert island and saved because some ship just *happened* to change course one day and saw them? What about those seagulls that came and ate all the bugs that were destroying the Mormons' grain, years ago? They built a monument to the gulls because of it."

"You're a spellbinder, you know that?" He put his finger on my cheek. "I like that dimple. . . . For a minute there you almost had me believing. But we don't need a change in the wind, or a good rain, or a ship, or a flock of gulls. We need a flock of people who'll change their vote. But they're so busy counting up what they'll make out of this deal, they wouldn't even feel an earthquake."

I opened my mouth to speak, and he kissed me, said, "No more talk," and kissed me again.

Eleven

I woke up so early Sunday morning that nobody else was stirring. The kids had been allowed to stay up later the night before, so they weren't awake. But I was so excited by yesterday's happenings, I think I was remembering them all night in my sleep. Faces went round and round before my eyes. There was Sharon's with the big dark eyes. (I didn't like to remember that stricken look.) I saw Josh's face as he leaned against the kitchen counter and told me I lacked the right brain cells, while he was probably thinking I lacked a lot more in looks, class, sophistication and so forth. June's face wore the smile of an angel while she said, "But we've got the clout, dear cousin."

And always there was Mac's face, changing from one mood to another.

I got up with the idea of jogging from the

house to the mailbox and back. I was in and out of the bathroom wihout a sound, tiptoed past Mac's closed door, and went down the back stairs. Walter's tail thumped on the kitchen floor, and I told him to stay, so he put his head down again. The cats were ready to go out and I knew it was all right for them to go.

The swallows were already active, and swooped down on the cats, who were used to them. Before I began my run, I sneaked around the house hoping to see a deer or two grazing in the orchard. I didn't see a deer. But I saw a fox.

In the ruddy glow of the rising sun, he was as red as a flame. His boots were coal-black, and his tail was a gorgeous, thick, furry plume as big as the rest of him. He trotted along, all business, and suddenly he stopped, cocked his head and stood listening, one forepaw lifted.

All at once he bunched himself up and sprang effortlessly into the air in a perfect, fiery arc. He came down with all four black feet together on whatever he'd heard in the tangled grass.

When I got back to the house everyone was up and the kitchen smelled heavenly with a special, leisurely, Sunday morning breakfast. "I wasn't here to help, so I'll do all the dishes," I said.

Mac wiped, but he seemed to be in and out of a dark cloud. I understood, because now that dark cloud was my business, too. He did put on a good act when the kids were around, the way he always did.

All nicely dressed for the occasion, we drove to church.

The tall steeple of this charming little country church was the one the children had shown me from Strawberry Hill. The setting was very pretty, and it would have been nice standing outside with Mac before the service if we hadn't seen the Jays the first thing. They looked wealthy and self-assured, like visiting royalty, and the older couple with them must have been the gentleman farmer and his wife, who behaved like the Lord and Lady of the manor.

"In *A Tale of Two Cities* they'd all be on the way to the guillotine by now," I said.

"They go to church to set a good example for the peasants," Mac muttered. His mother didn't hear that, she was talking to some other people. "Come on, let's go inside before they see us."

Too late. They were descending on us. The Elliot Thorntons were all gracious smiles, the Jays perfectly charming. Mrs. Thornton's manner was impeccable, but there was a flush in her cheeks.

They all sat at the back where we couldn't see them; Roger and Tabby liked to sit down front. But I knew that if I was conscious of them behind us, Mrs. Thornton and Mac must have been a hundred times more uncomfortable. Then, when the organ sounded a big chord for the first hymn, and the double doors opened and the choir was coming in, who was one half of the leading pair? *Sharon*.

I could swear that the only people *she* saw in that whole church were Mac and me, sitting side by side.

So between Sharon's doe-eyed stare from the choir loft, and knowing that the Jays were probably laughing to themselves about quaint little old Mac and Diana, I went through the beginning of the service without knowing much about it.

You never know when lightning's going to strike. It was right in the middle of one of the hymns, when we were all singing, "As it was in the beginning, is now and ever shall be," that I had my Idea.

It must have been there for some time. How could it *not* have been, considering the mother I had? But I'd been so fouled up with all my contradictory emotions that my creative impulse hadn't been given a chance to stir out of the murky corners of my brain where it lives.

I couldn't wait to tell Mac. It was a short sermon, but it seemed to go on for hours. Then there was a lot of socializing outside, and I was introduced to more people, whose names I couldn't remember a minute after I'd dutifully repeated them. There were some kids who went to school with Mac, and most were nice, but one of the girls gave me a frigid up-and-down glare and said pointedly, "I'm waiting for Sharon."

When we got home, everybody went swimming, so I still didn't get Mac alone. Then we had a late lunch on the table under the maples. After that it was the kids' quiet hour, and Mrs. Thornton said she had a headache and went to lie down. Meeting that bunch this morning must have been awfully hard on her.

I offered to clean up the kitchen, thinking Mac would help as he had this morning, but he disappeared, and I didn't know where to look for him. He'd taken Walter, so I had no way of tracking him. I lay on my bed and tried to read, but I was so jumpy I couldn't concentrate. When I heard a car driving in, I felt sick to my stomach, expecting the Jays and that so-called Gentleman Farmer. I rolled off my bed to look.

It wasn't the black and silver sports car, and the four people who got out were some I'd met outside the church; a youngish couple and one older pair. Mrs. Thornton had heard, and went out to welcome them. The kids hurried downstairs. "Where the heck are you, Mac?" I growled. "Look at all this time we'd have!"

But no sign of him. After a while I brushed my hair and went out to meet the people again.

The kids were playing out on the Magic Mountain; I could hear them shouting. The adults were having a pretty grim discussion. It broke off when I appeared. I was greeted kindly, and they asked a few questions to show a friendly interest, but I knew they were all seriously perturbed, and I was just in the way.

"Shall I make some tea?" I asked Mrs. Thornton, and she said, "Oh, Di, *would* you? Thank you very much!"

While I was setting up the tea tray, Mac walked in without a word and took a long drink of water. He stood staring out the window toward the woods while he drank.

"Mac," I said to his back. "Are you sorry about yesterday? I mean, do you wish it hadn't happened? I mean, with you and me?"

"No," he said promptly. He came and took me in his arms and kissed me. "But I just had to get off by myself. Those two showing up at church this morning, and Elliot with his smarmy smiles, calling me *son*! That headache of my mother's bothers me, too. She hasn't had it easy since my father died, but she felt there'd always be a roof over our heads. And now we're just waiting for the axe to fall, and having to keep up a front with the kids. I'm worried about her, Di."

The way he looked at me went straight to my heart. I hugged him with all my might.

"Mac, did you ever hear of historic preservation? What my mother doesn't know about it isn't worth knowing, and I've absorbed a lot without even trying. She's led and won some battles to save some old places. If you can prove a house is historically important —"

"Oh gosh, Di, this part of the state has almost more old places than new ones, so the house isn't that extraordinary."

"How about helping the slaves escape to Canada?"

"The Thorntons weren't the only ones to do that."

"There has to be something!" I insisted. "I feel it in my bones. I tell you, it struck me like lightning in church this morning."

"I suppose that makes it the real thing," he said sarcastically. "A message straight from headquarters."

I knew he had to be hard because he felt so defeated.

"Did George Washington ever stop here?" I asked. "Did they have secret meetings during the Revolution? Maybe the Thorntons headed some kind of guerrilla outfit to harass the British."

"If they did, they weren't the only ones."

"Well, look, will you at least *try* to find out something?" I begged. "You never can tell, and you won't feel as if you're just sitting still waiting for Doomsday. For starters we could pick the brains of those people out on the lawn."

"Pick their *brains*!" It was Roger coming in, all horrified fascination.

"It just means ask questions," I told him. "They might know some interesting things about olden times."

"Oh." I don't know if he was relieved or not. "Well, they're sure old enough. Great Uncle Matthew must be a hundred."

"Give or take thirty years," Mac said.

"Mother said to get out the cookies in the blue tin box," Roger said. He zoomed out again, making airplane noises.

I set out the cookies on a pretty plate, and poured boiling water into the teapot. "I wish your family had turned out a president, or even a vice-president. Maybe some senators and ambassadors, or famous generals or admirals. Or a hero like Nathan Hale. Or a great scientist. Don't you have one of them in the lot?"

"No Thornton," he said solemnly, "founded a famous college, discovered gravity, or the circulation of the blood. No Thornton invented the telephone, the steam engine, the electric light, or penicillin." He shrugged. "It's no use, Di."

"So you've already struck your colors, have you?" I said. "Well, we have not yet begun to fight, as somebody or other said. What are you doing after work tomorrow?"

"What do you have in mind?" he asked uneasily.

"Where are the family papers?"

"Not here. Over at the Historical Society, for safe keeping."

"Can I go and read them?"

"I guess so. Sure. It's upstairs in the library, and if I tell Miss White you're OK, she'll let you go up there. But they've been read a hundred times, maybe more. Deaths, births, crops, the weather, town meetings. war news, good and bad. . . . " He shrugged.

"But I'd like to see for myself. You can leave me there and take the kids somewhere for ice cream or something. I'll pay for it."

"It'll be just to humor you," he said, "because I know it won't be any good."

I gave him my sweetest smile. "Thank you for humoring me, dearest Mac. Nobody else does." I patted his cheek and he grabbed me and kissed me, and we were almost caught by Roger, Tabby, and Walter.

Monday morning Mac went to work a half hour earlier, so he could finish earlier. "I'm going to drive Di around and show her the sights this afternoon," he told his mother. "Such as they are."

Mrs. Thornton was pleased. After Mac left she said to me, "All he usually thinks about is work. I've been afraid he'd take on another job for the evenings, and he shouldn't, after he's been standing on a ladder all day."

It was touching, the way they worried about each other.

My lessons went well and then it was time for her to go, so the kids and Walter hopped into the station wagon for their morning ride out to the mailbox. I flipped to a clean page in my math notebook and began making a list of all the things we had to do this week. Making lists makes me feel efficient. You can't help but feel that all those crisply numbered items are going to pay off.

I was in the house while I did this, sitting on the front stairs. The house no longer sent me flying outdoors the instant I was left alone with it. Ever since I'd seen it as something that had to be protected I had loved it, and now I had the strangest feeling that it was loving me back. All the funny little creaks and ticks and odd thumps were its voice. It couldn't wag like Walter or purr like the cats, but it could show its feelings somehow.

Of course I couldn't tell Mac this. He'd think I'd freaked out for sure. He needed practical help, not burblings from a spaced-out female who thought the house was talking to her. I scowled at my list. It was much too short. What made me think I could find the magic words in material that had been read so many times? Just take the people who were here yesterday, for instance. I'd bet that Great Uncle Matthew knew most of it by heart, and the younger woman, his granddaughter, had edited some of the diaries for private publication just this year.

But I had this *feeling*! If only I didn't miss the one important clue — but what if I didn't look in the right place?

I'd have liked to poke around in the attic, but Mac said last night that he was positive nothing was up there that hadn't yet been discovered. He swore there was no secret hiding place between floors or behind a brick somewhere. With all the people who had grown up in this house, there couldn't have been an unexplored nook or cranny left.

"What about the stuff stored away in that room?"

"Forget it," he said. "It's mostly old furniture, and I went through that when I was a kid, looking for secret drawers. And the trunks are packed with things from the last few generations, including ours. And I've read all the old books. So there are no missing wills in them."

Still, I went up the stairs now, pressed down the thumb latch, and peeked in. I wouldn't have gone in without Mac anyway, that would have been bad manners, but I had to look. I didn't see anything but trunks and furniture and boxes. The mantelpiece over the empty fireplace was loaded with odd dishes and jugs and a row of oil lamps.

I heard the children coming, so I shut the door.

I was nervous as the day went on, for fear Mac would come home in a black mood and say my ideas were all foolishness. There were moments when I felt the same way, but then I'd stiffen my will.

He wasn't jovial when he came home, but he wasn't grim either. He sacrificed his daily swim for a quick shower, and I oversaw a quick wash and brush-up for the kids. I changed into fresh shorts and a top, combed my hair, grabbed my notebook, and I was ready.

We left Walter in the house, with a couple of extra dog biscuits as consolation, and the rest of us squeezed into the front of the pickup. Roger was between Mac and me, and I had Tabby on my lap.

Mac introduced me to the head librarian, who was a friend of his mother's, so I was free to go upstairs. I could have spent the whole day in that long room among the old photographs, newspapers, and books. And I love maps, even for places I don't know. But the Thornton papers were disappointingly few. The family came alive for me in them, but their quiet endurance, their griefs and joys, wouldn't be enough to save their house from those to whom the farm represented a huge, luscious slice of real estate.

When my hour was up, the pickup was waiting. Mac looked at me over the kids' heads with a question — hope against hope — and I shook my head, but tried to look optimistic at the same time.

"You were right," I said. "So I'm going to concentrate on something else."

"What?"

"I won't know till it hits me. I wish I were psychic. I could go through that house and get messages like crazy."

"What's that word mean?" asked Roger. "What messages?"

"Well, let's go!" Mac said heartily. "Hey, we haven't had ice cream yet! They wanted to wait for you. How about that?"

"Terrific!" I exclaimed.

We went into the drugstore for ice cream and sat on stools at the soda fountain. The kids were busy eating and looking around, so we could talk in low tones.

"Even if we could save the house," Mac

said, "it would be surrounded by Miles Thornton's blasted boxes, the barn gone and everything. I want it all left the way it is now."

" 'As it was in the beginning, is now, and ever shall be,' " I quoted. "That's what hit me in church yesterday." And when I repeated those words, the magic certainty came back to me. "Listen, when we do find something fabulously special about the house — and we're going to — nobody in their right minds would want to destroy its proper surroundings."

"Who says anybody in the bunch is in their right minds?"

There was no answer to that.

After croquet, with twilight coming on, Mac and I went canoeing. We didn't talk. I knew better than to chatter, but I wished I could reach him in his deep, hopeless, mood. The stars were reflected in the lake, and the loons' calls echoed hauntingly across it.

When we came silently ashore, we saw the white flash of a deer's tail as it leaped away. Suddenly Mac spoke for the first time in an hour.

"If you see a falling star, you make a wish. That never worked for me, so I have a new rule. When you see a deer, you kiss a girl."

And he did so.

Twelve

The next morning it was raining, which meant Mac couldn't paint. While I had my lessons, he was out in the barn repairing a chair, and the kids began making new cardboard houses for the shoebox village we'd built on the shore by the lake, since the other one would have been destroyed by the unexpected downpour.

After Mrs. Thornton left for work, Mac and I couldn't settle down to a private conversation, so we helped with the new houses. I made a bigger church with an even better steeple, and painted on some stained glass windows with Roger's water colors.

"It'll break my heart if this is ruined," I said. "We'll have to keep up with the weather reports and gather everything up when they promise rain."

Then we all went for hamburgers. I hadn't even touched my allowance yet, because Mac

wouldn't let me pay for the ice cream yesterday, but before we went into the hamburger
place I insisted on paying half of today's bill.

While we were eating, a couple of boys
came along and began talking to Mac. Tabby
was watching some little girls nearby and
Roger was chewing away and listening hard
to the older boys. I looked around, thankful
that none of the cute girls behind the counter
was Sharon, and I wondered idly what she
was doing this summer. Then I glanced out
at the parking lot. An elderly man was walking across it with some children. They all
looked happy.

He must be their grandfather, I thought.
Maybe their great-gramp. I'll bet he tells
them stories.

That's when it struck again, just as it had
in church. And again, I could hardly wait to
tell Mac. He'd introduced the boys, and it
looked as if they were going to hang around,
which was very flattering, but I had things
on my mind.

"Mac, do you know any old people?" I
asked him.

"I know about everybody in town. That's
Mr. Watson in the parking lot."

"I mean really old, but still clear in the
head. They're one of my mother's best
sources, because they often have stories from
way, way back, passed along by word of
mouth."

His eyes were alive, his whole manner had
changed. "Archie Gould," he said. "He knew

my grand-grandparents. He was their hired man for years, and he's told us all kinds of yarns about those days, and stuff they told *him*."

"Where does he live?"

"Way out at the end of a road we couldn't drive in this rain," Mac said sadly. "It will be a sea of mud."

"Well, can we go out there as soon as it stops raining? We could leave the truck and walk in, couldn't we?"

"Sure, but —" His shoulders slumped. "It's like the papers. If there was anything big, he'd have told us before now. We get our potatoes from him every fall, and he always talks, so we must have heard everything by now. And what could he say that would impress that bunch?"

"You never know."

"Never know what?" asked Roger suddenly. I wondered how long he'd been listening. "Hey, are we going out to Archie Gould's? Boy! He keeps goats, Di."

"I wish we could have a goat," said Tabby. "She could wear a bell and I'd call her Patty."

"I'd love to see the goats," I said, "but we can't go till it dries up a bit."

"Is that all you wanted to go for?" Roger asked shrewdly.

"Mostly to hear some of his old stories," I said. "I love things like that."

The rain stopped in the evening, and the next morning dawned warm and bright, and full of diamonds wherever you looked. The barn swallows seemed more energetic than ever, and of course so did Roger and Tabby. As for me, I was so excited at the thought of looking up Archie Gould that I had a hard time putting my mind on my work.

Now simmer down, Di, I told myself. *Don't count on hitting the jackpot now. You've been positive before, and look what happened. Nothing.*

We went down to the lake, cleared up the soggy remains of the ruined village, and laid out the new one. We added an airport, with a control tower made from a milk carton. It was really neat, and Roger's runways were practically professional. Tabby planted trees (seedling pines and spruces) along the main street, and gave the houses lawns made from clumps of bright green moss.

The whole scene was a masterpiece, if I do say so, and it kept me from anticipating the afternoon too much.

We had our lunch down there, and our quiet hour. I could have gone on reading peacefully when the kids resumed their play, but the tranquillity was interrupted by the sound of a car arriving at the house. We heard merry voices approaching, and Walter came proudly leading a procession of four. June was first, superb in an absolutely plain but perfect dark blue swimsuit. She was followed by a slim red-headed boy in trunks, then a girl in a striped suit, with dark hair tied up on top of her head, and then Josh, looking as handsome in swimming trunks as he did in his other clothes. They were all laughing and kidding.

"Here we are!" said June, like a hostess. "Isn't it perfect? Well, look who's here!" she exclaimed at the sight of us. "Some of the local elves."

"Hello, Princess Di!" Josh called. "And there's the little princess, too."

"And the little prince," said the dark girl to Roger. "How are you, sweetie? My, what big eyes. Is this your baby sister? What a doll!"

I was glad to see that Tabby backed off suspiciously.

June said lightly, "Di, this is Pam Raines and Davey Williams." They seemed nice. I might have liked them if they'd been with anybody else but the impossible Jays.

She and June went into the lake, looking like those willowy creatures in the low-calorie soft-drink commercials. Josh remained ornamentally ashore, giving us an eye-crinkling smile.

"You've got quite a layout here," he said. He set up the airport tower, which Walter had knocked down, and smoothed out the main runway, which someone had walked on. The kids began pointing out everything, talking at once.

"Di made the church," Tabby said. "See the steeple with the clock? She made that."

"And the stained glass windows, too," Roger said. "Now here's the town hall, and —"

"There's the school, right?" Josh was sitting on his heels, "I like the trees you've planted. Every village should have lots of trees . . . I see a farm out here."

"Yup, that's Mr. Morton's dairy farm," Roger said. "And here's his gravel pit. And here's the road from the woods to the docks."

"That's an impressive harbor." Still sitting on his heels, Josh looked up at me. "Any more problems with your math, Di?"

"Nope." I was curt.

"How's Cousin Mac? Still getting out of the wrong side of the bed these mornings? Or is he a grouch all the time?"

Roger, backing up a truck, looked up quickly and Josh said, "Just kidding, Roger."

"He's got plenty to be that way about." I gave Josh a long hard stare.

He put on a regretful expression. "If he'd have some common sense. . . . But no, he's one of those tough old Thorntons who hang on like bulldogs to the bitter end."

"Well!" I snapped. "If some tough old Thorntons hadn't hung on like bulldogs, there'd be nothing here for your bunch to —"

Roger's head came up, and darn it, I couldn't go on and spit out the rest of it. But Josh knew what I meant, all right. Those blue eyes narrowed. "Listen, babe, what I said about progress the other day is the truth. The old ones would be the last ones to say it was wrong. They'd realize that times have changed, and it's better that Thorntons make something off this place than strangers."

Roger was looking alertly from one side to the other. "What are you talking about? Why are you so mad, Di?" Tabby was listening, too.

"She's not mad, Roger," Josh said pleasantly. "She's just being serious. It looks good on her, too. She's sweet, and caring, and your brother's a very lucky guy."

"Why?" Tabby asked, perplexed, and Josh laughed. I knew I was scarlet. I could feel the heat, and I wished nastily that I could plant a foot on his chest, and push him over backward and then kick sand in his face.

"By the way," I said icily, "some people don't have any idea of — of current events, so please keep it that way."

He stood up and stepped across the village toward me. "Some people have to know sooner or later. The sooner the better, the way things are moving."

The arrogance of him! As if the bulldozers were already waiting by the mailbox!

"Don't be too sure," I said. "It may be *never*."

His eyes narrowed even more to sparkling blue slits. We stared at each other in silence. Suddenly he turned and sprinted out into the water to join the joyful noise of the other three.

"Josh is nice, isn't he?" said Tabby.

I wanted to be back at the house when Mac came, so he wouldn't be alone when he saw the sports car. "Let's ride out and meet Mac at the mailbox," I suggested. "I can take your mother's bike. She told me to use it whenever I wanted."

But they wouldn't budge, and there was no reason why they couldn't stay there; after all, they wouldn't be alone at the lake. It would be only for a few minutes anyway. I picked up the lunch basket.

Walter was torn betwen his duty to the kids and his desire to accompany the basket, but duty and "Stay" won out.

Thirteen

I was just in time. As the pickup came down the grade I could see Mac's scowl through the windshield. The truck rocked to a vibrating stop beside the sports car, and then he was out, and raging.

"What are they doing here?"

"They brought some friends to go swimming."

"What gives them the right to come barging in here, bringing their lousy friends, as if the place was already theirs?"

"You did say you couldn't keep them off the property," I pointed out. "Just out of the house. So they must feel they have a right."

"Sure, they have all kinds of rights, because they're in the majority, with the money and the power, and we're these quaint little fossils living in a quaint old house, so stupid we don't even know we're extinct."

His cheekbones were red. "What are they doing down there, planning a marina for a hundred boats, and where the gas tanks are going to be? And how fast they can clear out those pines?"

I tried to placate him. "So far they're only swimming. I told Josh not to say anything in front of the kids." I tried gentleness. "Come on, Mac. Let's gather up the kids and go looking for Archie Gould, as soon as you have your shower. Are you having a snack before or after?"

"I don't want a snack, and we're not leaving *them* on the place without supervision. They'll be through the house like — like —" He couldn't think of anything bad enough. He slammed the screen door behind him. I'd planned to run down and snatch the kids while he was having his shower, but the next thing I knew they, the Jays, and their guests were outside and ringing the bell.

"Hi," said Pam sweetly, giving Mac a limpid gaze.

Mac just stared at them.

Red-head Davey took her by the arm. "We'd like to look inside the barn. I'm interested in the construction."

"And I'm fascinated by this darling little house," Pam burbled. "I'd love to see inside while it's still standing."

"You couldn't very well see inside when it's a pile of rubbish, could you?" asked Mac with a ferocious grin.

"Oh, but they'll save all they can," she assured him. "The hand-hewn beams, and things. The old bricks could go for a great big fireplace in the clubhouse. Won't it be just fabulous?"

"So long, Pammie dear," said Josh. "Go look at the barn and don't stand directly under any swallows."

She and Davey walked off. Mac couldn't trust himself to speak and my own anger was making me sick to my stomach. Mac wheeled abruptly and went into the house.

Josh turned to me. "Can't you convince him, Di?" He sounded serious for once. "He'll be a lot happier taking part in the excitement than being stuck back there in the distant past."

"After all," June said, "it's not the end of the world."

"It is for more creatures than you know or care about!" I flared. I ran into the house.

Mac finally went up to take a shower and I made myself a cup of tea, my mother's remedy for calming the nerves. Mac's anger had upset me as much as the reason for it; it shut me out. I was no good to him whatsoever when he felt like that. I told myself that tonight we would take a walk, or canoe on the lake, and everything would smooth out again. Everything would be back to normal . . . No, *normal* meant, "As it was in the beginning, is now and ever shall be, world without end." And with Mac's world about to be destroyed, he had no room for me.

He came back to the kitchen in fresh

clothes and silently got a cold drink. I put my arms around him from behind and laid my cheek against his back.

"They've got so much," he said, "and we're nothing. We're like ants and they're kicking over our anthill and stamping on it."

"Ants don't share in the profits afterward." I tried for humor.

"For me it'll always be blood money," he said. I knew what he meant. I gave him a big squeeze around the middle and landed an awkward kiss somewhere near his ear, and he gave me a faint smile, so I thought I was getting through to him.

We sat down at the table, and just as I was expecting we could talk, Walter sounded off, and Mac went grim again. Darn that bunch, would they never stop meandering around here? Why didn't they have the common decency to stop needling Mac and clear out?

But I didn't hear their voices, and Walter was looking up the drive. Someone else was coming, and not in a car. Mac stared morosely at his soft drink, too depressed to care if an army marched in.

I went and looked, and saw two girls on bikes coasting down the grade toward the driveway. One of them was Sharon. The other was one of the girls I'd met at church, who'd given me a cold up-and-down inspection.

They both looked pretty determined as they glided into the shade of the maples. The sight of that expensive sports car set them back, I could see, and they craned their necks and stared around in all directions. But the glittering four had gone off through the orchard.

The girls walked their bikes toward the kitchen door. Sharon was bracing herself to be either brisk or casual, she wasn't sure which. I knew because I'd been in exactly the same position. You make up an excuse to go to somebody's house, and you hate yourself afterward, but you just have to go. *In case.*

"Sharon's here," I said quietly to Mac. Nothing from him, but Walter made friendly noises through the screen.

"There's old Walter!" Sharon said brightly. "Hello, Walter! Are you a good boy today?" Walter's tail beat against my legs. I went away from the door but Mac didn't take my place. He looked as if he hadn't heard a thing. Poor Sharon.

"Hi!" She peered through the screen. "Anybody home? Could we come in and have a drink of water? We've been riding for miles, and it's so hot, and this was the nearest place, so —"

She saw me and stopped short. "Hi, Sharon," I said. "Hi, Linda. Come on in." I got glasses out of the cupboard. "You can have soda if you want."

Sharon wet her lips. "Water will be okay. Mac, can I talk to you? *Alone?*"

"I'm going outside," said Linda with a

nasty glance at me. I shrugged. "So am I."

"*No*," Mac said. "Di stays."

"No, she doesn't," I said firmly. But I'd be darned if I'd stick with Linda. She took a glass of water and went out to the table under the maples. I went through the woodshed and made a fast trip past the barn, and climbed the Magic Mountain in the middle of the meadow. The barn hid the house, and it suited me to feel all alone in the world. There I sat on the warm granite, hugging my knees and feeling sorry for myself.

"You look like Little Sally Water sitting in a saucer," said Josh. He came up onto the ledge and sat beside me. "You know who she was?"

"I remember the game from kindergarten days," I said frigidly. "Don't tell me you still play it."

One golden eyebrow rose. "Mac frozen you out? Mighty self-centered, that lad."

"I refuse to discuss Mac with you."

"All right," he said amiably. "What shall we discuss, then?"

I'd have given anything to get him good and mad, he was so smug. "We can discuss how insensitive you are. You come in here like some mad surgeon saying, 'Now we're just going to cut off both your arms and legs, and it won't hurt a bit, you'll get along fine without them if you'll just be a good sport about it.' "

He grinned. "That's pretty extreme, isn't it?"

"No! And what do you or the rest of them know about this place? All those who've never stepped foot on it, but they think they've struck it rich? What do they — *you* — care about the wash from the big outboards destroying the waterbirds' nests? And taking away the orchard from the deer? And ruining the Forest Primeval?"

"The *what*? Where's that?"

"Across the lake."

"Now, Di, people will appreciate that forest," he said soothingly.

"How can they when it's gone, turned into suburbia? I'll bet you'd even bulldoze the family burying ground, too."

At last he was startled. "Believe me, Di, nobody will touch that."

"Probably because you're afraid of being haunted. Well, I wish you would be! I wish all those fancy places you're going to build will be so full of poltergeists smashing and throwing things that nobody can live in them!"

He wasn't smiling now. "About three hundred years ago I'd have thought you were a witch, Di, making evil spells."

"I wouldn't mind being one right now! I'd bewitch all the building equipment so nothing would work."

"If we have a flat tire on the way back to Elliot's, I'll know where the blame lies." He was kidding again, but the outburst had done me a lot of good. He went off whistling to meet the others.

Fourteen

I heard the sports car go, but I stayed where I was in case Sharon and Mac were having a real talk.

After a while Mac came out around the barn, shading his eyes as he looked across the meadow. Walter picked up my scent and led the way to the Magic Mountain. Pretty soon the three of us were on top of the ledge.

If Mac and Sharon had made up, I couldn't tell. "Can we go to Archie Gould's now?" I asked, as if everything was ordinary.

"Too late. My mother will be home pretty soon." He folded his arms on his knees and brooded into space.

"Why did you break off with Sharon?" I hadn't meant to ask, it just came out.

He shrugged. "We outgrew each other, I guess."

"*She* doesn't think so, Mac," I said bravely.

"If you made up with her today and don't know how to tell me —"

"You talk too much," he said, kissing me. After a few minutes of that, he said, "She had her drink and she left. That's all."

"Because you didn't speak one word to her, I bet. That's cruel, Mac Thornton. You could at least be honest with her."

"I *was* honest. I didn't have anything to say, so I didn't babble. Which you are doing right now." He kissed me with more determination, and it was very enjoyable. He'd gotten himself into a better mood by the time Mrs. Thornton came home.

The kids told her all about the visit, and how Josh had admired the village. They were both very much taken with him. She listened, smiling, and said, "That was nice." But she absentmindedly rubbed the back of her neck as if it ached. Mac saw that and his mouth went pale and tight.

We plodded through the usual evening things, staying off bad subjects, but I was depressed when I went to bed. The thought of Josh made me want to grind my teeth. I wondered if Mac was lying awake, too. I wished we could get up and go out in the warm night, and say all the things we hadn't been able to say earlier.

Then I thought of poor Mrs. Thornton. All her nights must be very bad now.

As if to mock us, the next morning was incredibly beautiful. Mrs. Thornton was pleasant as always, but seemed preoccupied and tired. There were shadows under her eyes. I told her that if she wanted to nap before she went to her classes we could skip my lessons, and I'd keep the children away from the house for a while.

"Thank you, Di, but I wouldn't sleep. I've too many things racing through my brain. It will help to work with you. I wish I'd had a chance to talk with Mac before he left this morning."

"You could drive around to where he's working," I suggested.

"Oh, he'd *love* that! You know how stiff-necked our Mac can be." *Our Mac.* It sounded nice.

After she left for the day, I tried to think of something special to do with the kids this morning. A hike around the lake to the beaver dam I hadn't seen yet? We could take our lunch.

I told the kids my idea and they were all for it. "I have a little washing to do. We'll go as soon as I finish," I said. They looked in the refrigerator to see what we could take for lunch.

I carried my laundry out to the line to hang it up, taking my time about it. There is something relaxing about washing clothes and pinning them on the line in the sun and fresh air, with birds singing. Dryers aren't half as nice.

When I finished and went into the house, Roger and Tabby had quite a bit of food spread out on the kitchen table. Roger was clever at sandwiches, huge unwieldy ones loaded with a complete meal. "I'll mix us up a gorgeous fruit punch," I promised.

The telephone rang and I went to answer it, hoping it was Mac. It was, of all people, my friend Kim.

"Are you out of your mind?" I asked after the first cries of delighted surprise. "This call will cost you the earth! Why didn't you wait until night?"

"I wanted to call you all last weekend, but I couldn't find the time. You wouldn't *believe* what's going on around here." A couple of weeks ago I'd have been dying with envy and homesickness as I listened to her news about my hometown, but now I was mildly interested, that's all. Even the scoop that Tom Latimer was going around with Beverly Lang couldn't wound me. Beverly worked as hard to charm as he did; they were both always on stage. "They deserve each other," I said. "I wonder who'll burn out first."

Kim laughed. "Tell me about the boy there. Is he okay?"

"More than okay," I put a lot into that, and Kim reacted suitably.

"Write me a long letter all about it," she commanded. "I can hardly wait. I suppose you can't talk now, with little kids around."

"That's right," I said, "and if I don't get back to them all the food in the house will be spread out on the kitchen table."

"They sound adorable," Kim said dryly.

I laughed. "Good-bye for now. Kim. Thanks loads for calling and I'll write."

"You'd better, or else," she threatened. "That place sounds unbelievable."

Free at last, I went back to the kitchen. No kids, no dog, but considerable debris. I began mixing assorted juices for the punch, and was busily stirring and tasting for several minutes before I realized that the house felt awfully empty. I shouted up the back stairs, but there was no response. So I took the bell from the kitchen mantel and went out and rang it. It sounded loud and clear through the summery hush, and echoed perfectly back from the woods.

I returned to the kitchen, expecting they'd return quickly from the tree house or the Magic Mountain. The first thing I saw this time was the large brown paper bag oddly decorated with a green marker pen and propped against the canisters on the counter. I'd missed it earlier. I went closer, and saw, in huge capitals, "DI ! ! !"

There was more printing, which I read with horror. It said: "We know there is SOMETHING WRONG, but nobody will tell us ANYTHING, so we have run away." It was signed with Roger's neat signature and Tabby's printed one. "P.S. This is FOR REAL this time. Love to all. R.T. and T.T."

Next: "P.S. Walter is with us so DON'T WORRY. We are SAFE." There was a row of x's, Tabby's kisses.

I have never fainted in my life, but my

head was spinning now and so was my stomach. I heard myself gasping, "No, No! They can't! What'll I *do*?"

Call Mac. Call Mrs. Thornton. Call the police. No, let the family decide on that. If the kids had gone out to the road they'd be easy to spot. But what about the old trail through the woods, that went all the way to Barclay?

I had chills, my teeth were chattering, my jaw was shaking. If only Kim hadn't called me — if only I hadn't let her run on —

I thought I was going to throw up. I remembered tales of large search parties, whole villages, Boy Scouts, police with tracker dogs, all turned out to find missing children who were never found again. Somehow I wobbled out into the hall, somehow my clammy trembling hand picked up the telephone, dropping it twice, finally getting it to my ear; a tremulous finger began to dial, and I kept swallowing so I'd be able to speak.

I heard a familiar sound behind me, but it took a few minutes to penetrate my fog of panic.

Dog toenails. A *ghost* dog? My scalp tightened, I looked around very slowly, squeezing the telephone against my chest, and saw Walter, just reaching the bottom step. He gave me his best doggy smile and came to me all wags. I set the telephone back and put my hands on the broad and very real head.

"*You*," I said, "are supposed to be with *them*." Keeping his eyes on mine, he wagged harder. "Where's Roger?" I asked him. "Where's Tabby?" He looked back at the stairs. "Find the kids," I urged him. "Come on, let's go and find Roger and Tabby. Let's go!"

He started enthusiastically for the stairs. I was right behind him. He led me straight to the storage room and scratched imperiously at the door. Not a sound from inside. He scratched again and looked up at me.

I pressed down on the thumb latch but I couldn't get the door open. Something had been put against it. "Well, Walter," I said loudly, "I don't think you and I can manage that extension ladder, but I'll call Mac at his job and he can come home and do it. We've got to get into that room, Walter, and see who's been moving things around. It could be burglars."

I raised my voice even more. "I have to call Mrs. Thornton at the college, too, and the police, and *everybody*, to find Roger and Tabby. I guess you didn't run away with them, did you, Walter? That's good, because maybe you can find them. Well, let's call up Mac. Wow, will he be mad!"

I walked away a few steps, stopped, and listened. Furtive stirrings inside, not mice, unless of a giant variety. Things were shifted, with a few thumps and scrapes. Then nothing. I counted sixty crocodiles, which make just one minute, though it seems much longer, then went back and tried the latch. This time the door opened.

Walter got in ahead of me, and zig-zagged among the trunks and cartons and furniture, straight to the cozy corner they'd made for themselves near the fireplace, picnic basket and all.

They looked up at me, brown eyes and round blue ones, as if they expected the sky to fall on them. Walter, immensely pleased with himself, washed their ears.

"Well!" I said. "I thought you two would be halfway to the next town by now. Where were you going from there?"

"We'd decide that," said Roger with dignity, "when we got there."

"I've a good mind to make you stay up here till Mac gets home! *Without* the picnic basket. Pulling a trick like that!" Walter lay down on the marble hearth, which must have been cooling to his furry belly. "Except by afternoon it'll be too hot up here, so I guess you'll have to stay in your rooms. We'll call it house arrest, since obviously I can't trust you out of my sight."

Roger's small jaw was set hard, his arms folded across his chest. Tabby, mouth drooping, twitched her shoulders and resumed picking at some loose wallpaper. I say "resumed" because she already had a little heap of scraps on the floor beside her.

"Boy, you were pretty brave," I continued. "All this stuff about running away for real this time, and you were right here in the house."

"We were going as soon as we could sneak

away," said Roger. "Then after you started yelling, and ringing the bell, that dumb old Walter kept fussing, so we had to let him out."

"That dumb old Walter has more sense than you have. Haven't you, Walter?" Walter woofed.

"Don't you love your mother and Mac?" I asked. Tabby sniffled a little and tore off a long strip of wall paper. But Roger was Stonewall Thornton. "Why are you angry with them, Roger?"

"Because they have secrets!" he exploded. "And we belong to this family, too! We should know!"

"Well, I guess I agree with you there, Roger," I said. He looked surprised. "But you ought to tell them straight out, like that, and not scare them to death first."

"Look!" said Tabby. "There's different paper underneath, it has violets on it. And there's more after that."

"Mama says there must be about ten layers of paper," Roger said, now anxious to change the previous subject. "Let's see." He got onto his knees, and started to peel away. I started instinctively to say, "No," and then I thought, *What the heck, somebody's going to kill the poor old house anyway.* And at least Roger had stopped worrying for a minute. So I hunched down beside them and said, "If we're careful we can see the other patterns. There must be some paper at the bottom over a hundred years old, at least."

Some of the layers stuck together and came off in thick wads, and I tried to separate these but just got crumbs and flakes. Roger worked patiently and cleverly. Tabby was less careful. But why tell her to take it easy? The house would forgive her; it was a loving house to its own.

"A wreath of roses," Robert said in disgust. "Didn't they put interesting things on wallpaper in those days?"

"You're expecting cars and airplanes?" I said.

"There's a cow!" said Tabby in pleased surprise. "And it won't come off!"

No wonder it wouldn't come off. Close to the fireplace a brown and white cow about six inches long gazed out at us from a green meadow. A painted cow in a painted meadow.

"Oh, my gosh!" We were all on our knees gazing back at her. Walter came over and pushed his big head between mine and Roger's. "Come on," I urged. "There must be more! But be careful — careful — easy does it."

I was my mother's daughter all right. All we had so far here was a cow, but she was the most fascinating cow I'd ever seen in my life, and she was not alone. There were other cows, grazing under a tree. And two horses, one black and one white. We picked and peeled until our fingers were sore. Tabby got tired and hungry and whiny, but I think Roger would have kept on as long as I did. But I had to call a halt. We took the picnic basket downstairs, washed our hands, talking all the while about what else there could be, and ate our lunch on the table under the maples. Then I ordained Quiet Hour, but I had a hard time concentrating on *A Tale of Two Cities*.

Tabby fell asleep, and awoke refreshed. We went back to work. I opened the windows and we left the door open into the hall, to make a breeze through. By mid-afternoon we had a strip cleared about six feet wide and as high up as I could comfortably reach. Tabby sat on the floor and worked along the baseboard. We had some blue water now, with ducks and geese on it, and in the foreground a bull moose with great antlers was standing up to his knees in the water. A bit of canoe was beginning to show.

"I hope it has Indians in it," said Roger tensely. "In war paint."

"They might hurt the cows," Tabby objected.

"They could be friendly. Just coming to show people how they used to look when they went to war."

"Oh, that would be nice," Tabby said.

"I hate to say this, kids, but we'd better start looking for Mac," I said. Walter had already left us.

"Are we going to tell him or surprise him?" Roger asked.

"Surprise me," said Mac's voice from the door and we all jumped.

Fifteen

Mac had read the note on the paper bag. *Walter is with us*, it said. But since Walter was peacefully snoozing on the cool kitchen floor, his coat tastefully decorated with shreds of ancient wallpaper, and our voices were floating down the back stairs, Mac recovered at once from his alarm. He had the bag in his hand when he walked in on us.

"What is the meaning of *this*?"

Roger blushed but looked his brother in the eye. "We changed our minds," he said. "Anybody can change their mind, can't they?"

"*Anybody*," said Mac, "can get into a whole lot of trouble around here, if *anybody* doesn't watch out." He turned to go. He looked hot, tired, and at the end of his rope.

"Mac, come and see my cows!" Tabby cried.

"Yes, look at what we've discovered, Mac," I said. "I don't know how much there is of it, but so far it's beautiful, and it seems to be very old. All this wallpaper has protected it, so the colors are still good."

He came and looked, and in spite of his depression, his eyes lit up. Then he shrugged and said, "So?" I wanted to put my arms around him and say, "Mac, I know, I know," but even if he'd allow me, it wouldn't help any.

"Wait till Mama sees it!" Tabby gloated.

"Going swimming?" I asked Mac. When he nodded I said, "Let's all go. We need a bath." The kids hated to break off, but I reminded them that tomorrow was another day.

I got a chance to speak to Mac alone at the lake. He and I were sitting on the dock dangling our feet, and the kids were wading around with their boats, not too close to us. I told him about this morning, and what Roger had told me. He groaned.

"So you ought to have a real talk with him," I said. "But don't let him know I told on him. He'll feel a lot better if it's just in the family."

Mac gave me a small weary smile, and put his hand around my arm. "Can I have a date tonight?" That from Mac in broad daylight, with the kids not twenty feet away! "We'll go canoeing by moonlight."

"It's a date. I'll go up to the house now," I said, "and you can have that little talk with Roger. Maybe you ought to include Tabby. Yes, I think you should."

He sighed. "I don't know how to begin."

"If only you could promise real ponies at the new place, that would help. They could have ponies, couldn't they? Out of your family's share of the big bucks?"

"I'll believe in those big bucks when I see them. And how long before they'd show up? Those ponies are just too far away to be any good to them now." His anguish nearly broke my heart. "What am I going to say to them?"

"Tell them the truth. Like 'Well, yes, kids, there are problems, but we'll lick them. We might have to move away from here, but it's not the end of the world and we'll all be together, and that's what counts.'"

He was slowly shaking his head, and the words clogged in my throat. He took my hand and squeezed it so hard it hurt, but if doing this helped Mac, the pain didn't matter.

"Hey, Di, you got something in your eye?"

Roger had waded out to his waist, a boat in his hand, and stood looking at us. "Mac's good at getting things out."

"I think it's gone now," I said.

"Good! Hey, Mac, Tabby and I've been talking. We want to keep the painted wall a secret till it's all uncovered, and then surprise Mother with it. She needs a nice big surprise like that."

"That's right, sport," said Mac. Here was the perfect time for me to leave the scene, and I started to get up.

"So anyway," Roger continued, "when we found that first cow and started looking for more, it made me feel more cheerful, and I thought if *you* helped us, it would make you more cheerful, too, and then when it was all done we could surprise Mother. Okay?"

He started his sailboat for the shore, wading after it and blowing to make a breeze. "I thought I was going to do the telling, but I just got told," said Mac.

"You going to help find the picture?" I asked.

"Anything to put off the evil hour. I may be a coward but I'm not lazy. Shall we put in an hour of it before my mother comes home?"

What a week that was! The kids were very good at keeping the secret. Roger wanted to spend all his time up there, but obviously they couldn't live indoors. I could have stayed there myself, it was so thrilling as the discoveries went on and on. We agreed to work on it in the morning, as soon as they'd seen their mother off, until lunch, and then not to go back until Mac came home. Then we'd get in about two hours of scraping.

Roger was steady; Tabby was surprisingly so for a six-year-old and didn't whine or fuss when she was tired of it, but went and played in her room or the attic. By the time Mrs. Thornton was due, we'd have had a dip to wash off the dust and flakes, and be ready to keep her company while she took her before-supper swim, if she didn't want to be alone.

The kids and I were picking wild strawberries in the meadow one hot noon when I looked up and saw Josh being escorted out to us by Walter. He looked very tall and his fair head was very bright as he came toward us. My stomach lurched unpleasantly at the sight of him. "Now what?" I muttered. "Talk about a bird of ill omen! Watch your feet!" I yelled. "Don't go tramping on the strawberries!"

"'Her voice was ever soft, gentle and low,'" he quoted. "'An excellent thing in woman.'"

"From *King Lear*," I snapped. "We read Shakespeare in my poor little underprivileged public high school."

"Don't be such a snob," he said. "I went to a public high school myself."

I felt foolish. "Excuse me, then. But watch out for the strawberries."

"I tread delicately as a cat." He brought out from behind his back a spray of five perfect little strawberries, and presented it with a deep bow to Tabby, who blossomed into dimples and giggles.

"Nothing I like better than a smile with two front teeth missing from it," said Josh. In spite of missing teeth Tabby neatly nipped the berries off their stems.

I couldn't tell the kids that Josh was the enemy. Right now he was the enchanter. He found berries as fast as they could in the tangled grass, and divided his share between their two dishes. "It smells good out here, doesn't it?" he observed, his face about two feet from mine. "Wild strawberries are really fragrant."

"Enjoy it while you can," I said. "I learned other poetry in school besides Shakespeare. There's one poem that says you should always look at everything beautiful as if this was your last chance, because there's always something or somebody about to steal it or destroy it."

He gave me a long hard look, and stood up. The kids were a little distance away, talking to each other, and Josh spoke in a low voice.

"The town officers are pretty happy about all the big taxes they'll be collecting. The soil-testers and environmental protection people will be coming next, but when they see our plans they'll know there's no danger of polluting the lake."

"Why are you telling *me*?" I asked. "Because you can't look Mac and his mother in the eye and tell them? Am I supposed to pass on the news? No way, Buster. *No way.*"

He tried that enchanter's smile on me. "The first time I saw you I thought, 'Here's a girl who knows which end is up. She knows that if you don't live in today's world, you're lost. But no, it turns out she's a bleeding heart who thinks more of squirrels than human beings.' "

"I just happen to think," I said with dignity, "that the human beings *you* represent don't need me to worry about them. You're not talking about housing for the poor and underprivileged, you're talking about something pretty fancy. So sure, I'm on the side of the squirrels, and the moose, and the loons, and this meadow, and the orchard. And the house. Don't forget the house."

"And don't forget Mac Thornton," he retorted hotly. "How fervent would you be for the cause if Mac Thornton wasn't up to his neck in it?"

"That's a foolish question. I wouldn't be here and know about it, if it wasn't for the Thorntons."

"Save me from a woman who always has to have the last word."

I laughed loudly. "Talk about the pot calling the kettle black!"

He tramped off, this time not watching out for strawberries.

"Hey, Di, is he mad?" Roger called to me.

"No, he's in a hurry, that's all."

I wouldn't have told Mac that he'd been here, but I knew the kids would, so while we were working on the room, I got it over with quickly. He had just discovered a church he recognized from some old photographs. It had long since burned down, but it had been one of the first meeting houses in the countryside after the Revolution. While I talked he kept saying, "Uh-huh. Mm-hmm — Wow, here's the weathervane!"

We were two-thirds around the next wall by now, over and past the windows. The painting gave us a bird's eye view of the whole countryside for miles around Hawthorne Farm. Cleared fields, stone walls, woods, animals, farmhouses, one stream with a sawmill, another with a grist mill where the farmers could take their wheat to be made into flour. There was the original village, with a blacksmith shop and a huge horse waiting outside, while another one was being shod near the fiery forge. And a tiny schoolhouse, with children around it. The colors had been miraculously preserved under those protective layers of wallpaper.

We were completely lost in that long-ago world as we worked, and always came back to today with a hard bump. Then Mac would be even more depressed except when we were in each other's arms, and even then the shadow of the near future lay coldly over us.

We were always glad to return to the painted world again, where nothing else mattered but the next wonderful discovery to be made. Working side by side with Mac, not needing conversation because we'd have time alone before bedtime, sometimes the thought of Josh needled me, but I'd fight it off. It didn't belong here. This was our private planet, innocently shared by Roger and Tabby, and the four of us keeping the secret. Mac and I shared another secret of course; that we were doing this only to see what was there, because the painted room was doomed. We wouldn't talk about that even when we were alone.

The weekend would be difficult. We impressed it on the kids that if they want to save the surprise for their mother, they mustn't go near the room for those two days. We'd all do other things and pretend nothing was going on. But Roger was keen. "What if she happens to go up there for something?"

"All we can do is hope that doesn't happen," Mac said.

"But if it does," I said, always the optimist though sometimes it was difficult, "she'll have the surprise now, and with half the room done it'll be a good one."

That was one of the longest weekends in my life; Mac worked on Saturday to make up for the rainy day when he'd stayed home. We had a cookout at the lake that night and sang songs around our little fire well into the twilight, until the kids were yawning and leaning heavily on the nearest older person.

Such an evening was like the wild strawberries and the barn swallows, who wouldn't be there next year.

Sunday afternoon Mac and I took the canoe across the lake and I walked for the first time in the Forest Primeval, which was not gloomy but grand. Back at the house there was a meeting of the local holdouts.

"I should be there, I suppose," Mac said, "but what good is talk? It just keeps me so riled up I want to be violent." He looked up at the tall old spruces hung with streamers of gray moss. "I'm going to keep looking at everything as long as we have it."

"Mac," I began, "no matter what happens, we know each other now, and that will go on, won't it?" My mouth was dry, because he kept his face turned away from me. "I mean, everything won't come to a screeching halt, will it? When I have to go back home, that won't be the end. I mean, we'll still —"

I was falling all over myself, and he was no help. *Diana, stop right now!* I commanded myself, but I couldn't stop. "We'll see each other every chance, won't we? Call up, and write, and we could visit in the winter . . . wherever you are."

He looked around at me, his eyes very green under the black forelock. "The end of summer's a long time away," he said harshly, "but it's still coming too fast. So if you don't mind, I don't want to talk about *afterward.*"

And that was that.

The next day we had a thick fog, no good for painting houses, so Mac stayed home. The instant Mrs. Thornton left, Mac and I went upstairs to work. We had a little while alone, because the children had gone with her to the mailbox. Mac had insisted on this each day, when the kids were so anxious to start scraping. "Otherwise Mother will suspect something," he said, and Roger understood that.

Now in our twenty minutes or so alone, we worked in silence, separated from each other by more than the collection of trunks and old furniture that we'd pushed and dragged into the middle of the room, away from the walls. He'd hardly spoken this morning, and I was beginning to feel a comradeship with Sharon.

Then all at once he came to stand behind me. "Let's see how you're doing," he said. He turned me around and kissed me, and before I could kiss him back we heard Walter barking downstairs, and the kids' light, high voices. I kissed him back anyway, good and hard, just as the thundering herd hit the front stairs.

"*See?*" Tabby cried in triumph. "Yeah, look!" Roger shouted.

Josh Thornton stood on the threshold. He looked absolutely stunned.

"What in heck are *you* doing here, Thornton?" Mac demanded. Even his ears were scarlet, and his eyes were like green glass.

Josh didn't seem to hear. He was gazing at the painted walls like someone who'd walked into a cave full of diamonds. You could hear his hard breathing, as if he'd just run a stiff race. "Look at this place," he almost whispered it. "I had no idea — did *you?*" he asked Mac, who didn't answer.

"No," I said. "Nobody did. We found out by accident."

"I found that cow," Tabby stated with pride, putting her finger on it. "I named her Clover."

Josh moved like a sleepwalker around the trunks and furniture. "You've uncovered two walls already. Is the whole room painted, I wonder?"

"You two," Mac addressed Roger and Tabby. "You've kept this from our mother.

How come you spill it out to *him*?"

"Because it's a surprise for Mother," Roger said simply. "Not for him."

"It's a surprise for me, too, chum," Josh said. "It's knocked me end over end. It's — it's *tremendous*!" His eyes were shining. "Look at those colors! Fresh as spring. Look at the detail! Hey, isn't that the mill creek that runs through Elliott's place?"

Mac said quietly, "Now that you've looked, would you mind getting out?"

Don't let this all be spoiled for us because Josh has seen it, I was praying as I watched them.

"I love this little dog," Tabby said.

"Hey, Josh," Roger clamored, "see this big black bull? He's pawing the ground and looking at that man in the red shirt."

"Would *you* mind," Josh asked, as quietly as Mac had spoken, "letting me help? I'd consider it an honor."

"To get ahead of the wrecking crew?" Mac asked harshly.

"Yeah," Josh said. "In more ways than one."

"Come on down and get your lunch, Mac," I said. "Let's go, kids."

He looked at me as if I were crazy. "And leave *him*?"

"He can't very well steal it. Come on." My heart was pounding, and I was sweating. I didn't expect him to follow me, but he did. In the kitchen I said, "Everybody wash up," and they did so at the kitchen sink.

"What is it with this guy and you?" Mac glared at me.

"I feel the same way as you do about him, but how are you going to get him out without a fight?"

"Blabbermouth," Mac said bitterly to Roger.

"Well, you never said not to tell *him*."

"In case you never noticed, that is the way children are," I said to Mac. "They always pick out the one important item you forgot to mention, and do it and say you never told them not to. Roger and Tabby, set the table. We have egg and tuna salad, I believe."

"Are you going to make lunch for Josh, Di?" Tabby was all radiant.

"No, I am not."

"You're so full of suggestions," Mac said, "how do we get rid of him? He'll stick like a burr or porcupine quills."

"We'll think of something," I said with false confidence. "We'll appeal to his better nature."

"What makes you think he has one?"

"*I* think he's handsome," said Tabby.

"I like him, too, and he's our cousin," said Roger.

They were all set to gallop through their lunch and rush upstairs, but Mac told them they might as well take time to chew, because they couldn't skip the quiet hour.

While I ate I wondered if I *could* appeal to Josh's better nature. Tell him this was a little private family project, a kind of farewell to the house, and important for Mac and the kids to do together. It was taking up the kids' minds, and helping Mac, too, because he was so depressed. No, that would be disloyal to Mac, talking about him like that. But surely if I asked Josh nicely not to barge in where he wasn't wanted — No, that didn't sound good either.

How about telling him straight out that as one of the invading army he could at least keep away until the surrender was official?

Mac didn't say another word during lunch. Afterwards he sent the kids to their rooms with strict orders to stay there for one hour.

As he and I started up the stairs and heard Josh whistling the way people do when they're absorbed in what they're doing, Mac set his jaw and slitted his eyes. I seized his arm. "Mac, no matter how mad you are, don't hit him."

"With my luck, he'd probably be a Black Belt."

"I was thinking about Roger and Tabby. They'd be scared stiff, and your mother would have to know, and —"

"I know, I know. He's got me between a rock and a hard place, and I could happily kill him for it, but I'm not allowed to even bloody his nose."

I took his face between my hands and kissed him. He was rigid at first and then he relaxed and kissed me back. We held hands as we went the rest of the way. Almost to the top he stopped us, and gave me a long, desperate look.

"How do we do it, Di?"

"Just say you'd rather he didn't help out. He's not absolutely obtuse, he knows how you feel about everything."

Josh greeted us joyously. "Look what I just found! Two guys racing horses!"

Did I say he *wasn't* obtuse? Here he was, laughing and talking as if we were all buddies. "I've been looking for a signature, but I guess you haven't come to it yet. It's important if he signed it."

"Why?" Mac was chilly and distant.

"Because murals like this are genuine folk art, and some of the painters were better than others. This man is terrific, doing all this from a bird's eye view! Perfect perspective! It's like having perfect pitch."

"What difference does it make?" Mac asked. "A year from now there'll be a swimming pool here."

"Are you *crazy*? No, I take that back. No offense meant, Mac," he said soberly. "*We're* the crazy ones. Or we will be if we don't —" For the first time I was seeing Josh Thornton having trouble expressing himself. "Listen, I'm going to get June, okay?" He was on his way out of the room.

"No, it's not okay!" Mac shouted after him, but he was running downstairs.

Then we heard Roger calling from his window. "Hey, Josh, don't bring her when our mother's home!"

Sixteen

Mac said with dangerous softness, "I'm going out for a long walk in the fog." And he went. I was dying to go with him, but someone had to stay with the children, and I did have some work to do for tomorrow's lessons.

I had a hard time doing my work. Would the Jays come or wouldn't they? It was downright cruel that Mac and I couldn't have this special time together. How could I make it clear what they were doing to us? I hated the picture of Mac out there alone and brooding; and I couldn't help thinking that no matter how close we held each other sometimes, I could never be *that* close.

Mac was back by two, still silent but intent on working. We were now opposite the fireplace. Josh had uncovered quite a bit while we were at lunch, and the children were thrilled with the impromptu horse race. But as each of us discovered some new enchanting bit, we completely forgot about the Jays. We were lost in that old, but still new, landscape.

Mac and I were working together on a waterfall. "That's in Beechwood Gorge," he said. "I'll take you there. It hasn't changed any."

Out in the hall Walter growled and went downstairs. When he began to bark it wasn't hostile. "Hey, Josh must be back," Roger exclaimed. He shot out of the room, Tabby behind him.

"Careful on the stairs!" Mac called after the kids. He gave me a disgusted look. We heard the glad sounds of welcome down in the kitchen, and a girl's laugh.

"Yep, that's old June, I reckon," I said.

"I'm going out the front door," said Mac.

"No, you aren't!"

"If I can't belt *him*, and I can't insult *her*, why do I have to stand here and look at them?"

It was too late anyway. The kids came scrambling up the stairs talking a mile a minute, the Jays following.

"This had better be good, Joshua," June said languidly. "Whatever it is."

"It is, it is!" he assured her.

I put my arm around Mac's middle, and he held me tightly, as we watched the Jays come in. If Josh had been struck speechless, June looked hypnotized. She moved as if in a trance, and in her wonder she looked really beautiful.

"It's — it's — words aren't good enough! It's *stupendous!*" She walked slowly all around the room through the shreds of old wallpaper, looking at everything, smiling, murmuring to herself, sometimes delicately touching. "And you've been so careful, all of you," she marveled.

"I helped," Tabby said proudly. "I love to peel off wallpaper."

"There's nothing more handy than a good wallpaper peeler," June said.

"If it's signed," Josh said, "it must be at the end, wherever that is. Maybe on the other side of the fireplace. Do you know anybody who'd —" He stopped.

"Yes." She came back to us. "Can I help?" It was direct.

"It's our project," Mac said stiffly. "Mine and the kids', and Di is in it, too, because she discovered it."

"Only because Tabby can't leave loose wallpaper alone."

"It's a surprise for our mother," Roger explained. "I already told Josh."

"It will be a gorgeous surprise," June told him. "Josh and I want to help, that's all. Please," she said to Mac. "I know how you feel about us, but *please.*"

"When I said I'd be honored, I meant it, Mac," Josh said.

"Please, Mac." Roger's brown eyes beseeched. "Then Mother can see it sooner."

"Oh, I can't wait!" Tabby hugged Mac's legs. "Please, Mac?"

He bit his lower lip. Everybody waited in suspense.

"All right," he said finally. "But I'd like you to leave before my mother gets home."

"Just give us a time limit," June urged.

"Five."

"Five it is," said Josh.

Well, it was incredible. All the contempt and the enmity were buried for the time being while we worked together. Mac was terribly tense at first. I know, because I kept right beside him, and I also knew when he began to relax and lose himself in what he was doing. Roger worked quietly, and only Tabby talked.

The Jays were silently absorbed. I sneaked a look at them, and it was like seeing two serious and dedicated strangers. I imagined them bent over their drawing boards in college and then in the family firm.

But Mac had had to stop thinking about his career, and he was ready to give up his college money; he and his mother had argued about it last night after the kids went to bed. So I resented the Jays' dedication, because they were secure in it and Mac could not be. He wanted to have this place, and he was about to lose it.

When the grandfather clock downstairs struck five, June said, "Time for these two Cinderellas to split." The kids giggled appreciatively. "So long, everybody," Josh called on the way out.

Mac didn't look around, but I did, for manner's sake. "Oh. So long."

Josh winked at me. "Princess Di, should I back out of your presence?"

"Only if you want to fall over Walter."

"Come on, Josh," June said from the stairs. "We said we'd git, so let's git."

"See you tomorrow!" Josh said, and vanished. The kids went with Walter to see them off.

"Never even asked if I'd let them come back," Mac growled. "They're taking it away from us, the way they're taking everything."

"No, they aren't," I said. "I mean, not this project. We'd done over half of this when they first saw it, and then they begged, they really pleaded. So you're granting them privileges."

"We'll lock 'em out tomorrow. I don't owe them any generosity."

We spent the foggy evening around the living room fireplace with games and music. I went to sleep imagining myself one of those figures that walked along the paths in our painted world. I was up early to go out to the barn with Mac in a fair morning, with the swallows chattering and diving around us.

"*Courage, mon ami*," I said, kissing him on both cheeks like a French general. He gave me a valiant grin and a muscular hug.

As soon as they'd seen their mother off, the kids began looking for the Jays, and talked about them constantly as we worked. It was too bad that one day they'd have to realize that these charming, wondrous creatures were The Enemy.

They came after lunch, and Roger and Tabby were beside themselves. I could see there was no point in insisting upon a quiet hour. They chattered away to June who, if she wasn't really fond of small kids, was putting on a good act. She kept working all the time, however. Josh came over to me.

"Did you have anything to do with the truce?"

"Mac makes up his own mind," I said loftily. "Besides, why should I try to do you any favors?"

"In this case," he said without smiling, "you might be doing favors for somebody else. Maybe even Mac. Who knows? Anyway, this is the kind of experience a person can expect only once in a lifetime, if at all, and I'm thankful for it." He sounded almost humble, and I couldn't believe it.

I worried over how Mac would feel about their working here without him. It would look as if I were getting friendly with The Enemy behind his back. But, as usual, the lovely world on the walls embraced us, and everything else was forgotten. Roger quieted as he settled down to work, and soon Tabby was the only one talking — to herself and the nearest cat.

When Mac came home, he didn't come near the painted room before he went to shower and change, and I was on pins and needles for fear he wouldn't appear at all. I was about to go looking for him when he showed up. Evidently he had remembered that he was granting the privileges, so he had better behave as if he believed it.

"Hi, Mac." "Hello, Mac." "How goes it?" Absentminded greetings from preoccupied workers. Tabby dragged him to a corner to see a rail fence along the baseboard, with a family of owls sitting on it.

"Aren't they perfect?" June asked. "Mac, this is your project, so one of you should discover the signature."

"What's so important about it?" Mac was surly. "What does it all come to in the end?"

"This painting is fabulous, no matter who did it. To Josh and me, it's reason enough for — well, never mind that now. But if it's signed by the person I hope signed it, that will impress an awful lot more people."

I was beginning to have gooseflesh. *Go along with her, Mac,* I silently prayed. *You've gone this far, just keep on.*

Finally he shrugged. "Where do you think it is?"

Josh thought it would be at the opposite side of the fireplace from where we began. But he was wrong. The mural never ended. It ran straight across the mantel and joined onto the scene at the other side, where Tabby had found Clover.

The scene over the mantel was a portrait of this house, which is why we hadn't found it anywhere else on the walls. No maple trees grew on the front lawn then, but there in a double row, sitting and standing, were the people who must have lived in the house when the painting was made. Children sat on laps or on the ground, holding dogs and cats. Horses watched over a fence. A black sheep, a lamb, and some large red hens wandered through the foreground. Everywhere you looked there was some new treasure. Tabby and Roger stood up on chairs to see, and they were struck mute with ecstasy. The rest of us were speechless, too.

Tabby's forefinger reached out and touched a white rabbit the rest of us hadn't seen. It was busily eating the tops of some flowers at the bottom of the scene. Then the finger moved along into the flower bed. "That looks like printing."

The letters were artfully tangled in among the stems. June put her arm around Tabby and said, "Let's spell it out together."

It was a name. *Angela Mason.* It was followed by a date. *1815.*

June let out a whoop that bounced back from the ceiling. June, the cool, suave, and sophisticated, was hugging Tabby, hugging Roger, hugging Josh. "It is, it *is*! Oh, if it's only genuine! But it *has* to be! I couldn't stand it if it wasn't!"

I even let her hug me because I was infected by her joy, and if she couldn't hug Mac, she gripped his shoulder.

Josh held out his arms to me. "I ought to get in on all this!" I backed off, and he laughed aloud. *Jubilant* was the word to describe him.

"What's all this about?" Mac demanded over the uproar.

"It's something wonderful, that's all!" said June. "Can we use your telephone? Josh, get out your credit card. I'll call Phil Abbott to get right out here to authenticate this."

"Let me get Dad first," Josh insisted. "It can't wait."

The kids chased them downstairs, while Walter barked impartially at everyone.

"I never even said they could use the phone," Mac said.

"I think we'd better let them use it." I was shivering, and he put his arms around me.

"What's the matter? Are you sick?"

"No, but — oh, I can't put into words the way I feel. Let's just wait and see."

From the head of the stairs we heard Josh telling his father to hold everything, and not to dare miss coming for the weekend. We heard June telling the mysterious Phil that he must come out from Boston as soon as he could, and he was not to tell a soul about this errand.

"You will be thrilled to the marrow, Phil," she said. "I give you my solemn oath."

Then they left, saying they'd see us soon. We were completely winded, but at the same time so keyed up it was impossible to settle down. The children were utterly wild, and Mac immediately decreed a long hike, so they'd use up all their surplus energy before their mother got home.

As they charged off ahead of us we caught each other's hands and lightly laced our fingers. "I want to look at it again," he said to me. "Just quietly, with you. I didn't have a chance to take it in, with those two whooping around. What do you think is going on?"

"What I think is — well, we never did get to see Archie Gould and find out if he knew something important about the house, but Clover may just possibly turn out to be the Cow of the Year."

Seventeen

Later that evening, Mac and I sneaked upstairs to look at the painted room alone. In the cool north light the colors shone softly. One of my favorite poets used the phrase "All a wonder and a wild delight," and that's what this place was. Hand in hand like the Babes in the Wood, Mac and I wandered through an eternal springtime, coming back each time to that group over the mantel.

"This house has ghosts all right," I said. "It's these people. They've been waiting all these years to be discovered. Mac, the house *knew*."

He gave me a sad and very adult smile. "I wonder if the house knows it's doomed. I almost wish we hadn't found this. It makes it worse, if anything could be."

"Nobody can destroy this," I said stubbornly. "Somebody hid it once, but it survived."

"You're a dreamer, Di." He kissed me. It was a quiet and reflective kiss. "I think I know who most of those people are. Joshua Thornton lived here in the early 1800s. Old Josh. *That's* a laugh, isn't it? With young Josh ready to tear it down."

"The way he acted this afternoon, I don't think —" But I didn't get any farther.

Mac went on. "You know, everybody in the gang who wants to tear up the place is descended from somebody in that picture, or they're married to a descendant. And here the family sits for a portrait, at least three generations of them, proud as heck, knowing they've got their land no matter what, and *I* feel as if we've brought 'em back to life just to put 'em in front of a firing squad." He dropped my hand and walked out of the room.

After dark, we sat on the back doorstep, but Mac was too quiet when he said goodnight, and this sadness in him was something new, more disturbing than anger.

When something terrible or wonderful has happened, you always remember it before you wake up in the morning, and that's how I woke up the next day. To me it was still wonderful and no reason for sadness. If only I could convince Mac. But he wasn't about to trust the "feeling in my bones."

Sure, that feeling had convinced me there was something extraordinary about the house, and there *was*. But, as Mac would say, so what? He seemed to feel worse than before, and if I let myself go along with that, I'd have been sunk. But I just couldn't admit the possibility that the painted room could be destroyed.

There's nothing like having to concentrate on geometry and Latin grammar to bring one down to earth. In spite of being at a constant boil inside, I was doing my work well. *A sign of maturity, Diana,* I told myself in my principal's deep voice, and smiled modestly. Smugly, too, I'm afraid.

After Mrs. Thornton left for work, I kept expecting the telephone to ring, but it didn't. Considering the way the Jays had raced out of here yesterday, after making their frantic telephone calls, their silence was deflating.

The minute the kids arrived back at the house they raced upstairs to look and gloat. I put them to work sweeping up the mess underfoot, while I washed the mantelpiece, the windowframes, and the door. I put the finishing touches to the floor, wiping up the dust with damp cloths. (There was a well-stuffed ragbag in the attic.)

We carried the boxes of debris out to the barn for Mac to burn in the incinerator. Then we went down to the lake and splashed around in the water enough to clean ourselves up without breaking the no-swimming rules. I shampooed the kids' hair down there, which they thought a great improvement over the kitchen sink.

I had a strong feeling that Mrs. Thornton was going to see the painted room tonight.

The kids couldn't wait for the weekend.

Mac came home, and still no Jays. We went swimming then, and I told him on the q.t. that the kids weren't going to be able to keep mum much longer. "They're bursting," I said. "Why wait for the weekend? Why not to-night? You don't know what the weekend will bring."

"Yes, I do. Miles Thornton with his plans and a way to save the painting. *That's* what those two were excited about yesterday. Getting this 'genuine folk art' intact to a museum, before they wreck the house."

This gave me cold chills. What if he was right? All my optimism went and I was not only cold, but sick. A nippy wind sprang up and ruffled the lake, and dark clouds blew over like doom. The kids began to turn faintly blue, so Mac ordered them up to the house. They didn't protest, for once.

We'd all gotten dressed and collected in the kitchen for a warm drink when the Jays drove in. They had a man with them, a long, skinny person with a thin beard and thick glasses. His name was Philip Abbott. He had a pleasant voice and manner.

"This is very good of you to let me come," he said to Mac when they shook hands. Mac had this funny quirk to his mouth as if he were about to say, "I've got nothing to do with it. Those two took over."

But he didn't say anything. "Roger and Tabby, will you show Mr. Abbott the way?" June asked, and they escorted him to the front stairs. Mac at last showed expression: surprise. "Aren't you going up with him?"

"He prefers it this way," June said. She was actually nervous, twisting her fingers, biting her lip. Josh was unusually quiet for him.

"What are you jumpy about?" Mac asked June. "I didn't think anything could shake you up."

"This does."

"Why? It shouldn't stop the swimming pool."

"Will you shut up about that swimming pool?" she burst out. Josh laughed.

"Mac, if your stomach's been churning with hatred of us, you're having your revenge. Now *we're* in a state, to put it mildly." He laid his hand over mine. It was cold. "Feel that clammy paw? Nerves. Bet you thought I didn't have a nerve in my body, didn't you?"

"Shut up, Josh, you're babbling," said his sister. "Save your strength for what we have to do."

The kids came back. "He wants to look at it all alone," Roger announced.

"Okay," Mac said. "You two buzz off. Go swing, or check out the tree house, anything as long as you stay out till I call you."

"Anything but run away," I added, and Roger twinkled at me.

"No way! Come on, Walter."

When they'd gone, Mac stood in front of the fireplace and spoke quietly. "What do you have to do? Seeing as my family's about to be booted out of the house after taking care of it all these years, I have a right to know."

Josh opened his mouth, but Mac overrode him. "Let me guess. You want to save those murals. Cut them out of the house before it's pulled down."

"Cut them out?" Josh was astonished. "Man, you're so far out it'll take you years to get back to earth!"

"Where do you figure on putting them? In a museum? Or in your classiest condo?"

Josh shook his head as if mosquitoes were biting him. "Listen, Mac —"

"Here he comes," June said tensely, standing up.

Mr. Abbott came in, wiping his forehead. "Look at that." He held up a shaking hand. His voice was unsteady, too. "I'll put you all out of your misery. The painting is authentic. There's no doubt that Angela Mason did it. Come up and I'll show you the little touches that nobody else could duplicate. Her animals, for instance. Her humor. And the number of layers of wallpaper over it, and the age of the first layer, prove that this could not be a forgery."

Josh glanced at me. "I saved fragments as I worked, and numbered them. Sneak that I am."

"Besides," Mr. Abbott continued, "she was known to have painted the front parlor in the famous Daventry house, not too far from here, in 1814."

"I've seen that room," Mac said unexpectedly. "Our art class visited it last year." He was pale, as he always was when under great stress.

Mr. Abbott said, "Your family must have had position and some spare money to be able to afford her. She wasn't like the wandering painters who turned out portraits for their meals and lodgings."

"But why didn't somebody write something about it?" Josh asked. "Enough people have been through the family papers to catch any reference to it, if there was one."

I wet my lips. "I haven't read everything," I said bravely, "but I remember one letter. Someone said that a little girl took after her Grammie Angie. They said, 'She's real clever about colors and at making up scenes to embroider. Maybe she'll be an artist, too.' "

They all stared at me. I stumbled on. "Maybe Angela Mason m-married a Thornton and became a farmer's wife, and —"

"Then quite possibly this is the last set of murals she ever did!" Mr. Abbott finished, waving his glasses in excitement. "If you're right, my dear," he said to me, "she should be in the painting, too, but we'll never know. Even if the name is just a coincidence, and Angela Mason *didn't* marry into the family, she certainly did that magnificent work. However, if she lived in this house and became your ancestress" — he nodded at the three Thorntons — "what a wonderful inheritance!"

Those three were slightly stupefied. I was the only one besides Mr. Abbott who still had all my wits about me. "I wonder why it was ever covered up," I said. "Who'd want to hide something like that?"

"You'd be surprised," he said. "Someone might have thought it was too old-fashioned, and that wallpaper was a lot more classy and modern. There's been many a lovely thing hidden away because of that. In this case, the miracle is that it was discovered and in such good condition."

Miracles, Mac, I thought. *We wanted a miracle.*

"Will you have a cup of tea, Mr. Abbott?" I asked, as the other three were still silent.

"It's all very tempting, but I must get back to Boston. If I stayed fifteen minutes longer, it would break my heart to leave that jewel of a room upstairs. And what a perfect setting for it out there!" He waved his hand at the windows. "Flawless!"

I was watching Mac. Suddenly he walked straight out of the room, out of doors, and didn't look back. Walter ran after him. They disappeared around the far end of the house, and it was as if they had gone forever.

Mac didn't want me; after all we'd been to each other, he had no room for me. Perhaps he blamed me for the discovery of the painted room. I needn't have gone along with Tabby when she scraped away enough paper to uncover Clover. I should have stopped her then and there.

"Can you two be trusted for about a half hour?" I asked. "While I lie down and try to get rid of a headache? Your mother ought to be right along."

"Sure, you can trust us, Di," Roger said authoritatively. "We won't do anything we shouldn't."

"Thanks." I ran upstairs, and was crying before I got to my room.

Eighteen

The kids had had it; there was no way we could get through dinner that night without showing Mrs. Thornton the painted room. They did manage not to tell her what the surprise was. As they convoyed her toward the stairs like two little tugboats, with Mac following dourly behind, I grabbed one of his jackets from a hook in the kitchen and slipped out the back way. Dear old Walter went with me. That was so nice of him I felt like crying again, but I didn't want Mrs. Thornton to know about it, and certainly not Mac.

Then I thought hopefully that he might come out to look for me, and he'd tell me he didn't blame me for anything, and he was truly glad that I was here for him this summer.

But he didn't come. Of course he didn't know which way I'd gone, I reasoned. Somebody rang the bell for me, and Walter urged me to hurry back to the house. He knew the bell meant food.

Mrs. Thornton had a girlish blush burning on her cheekbones, and her eyes were wet and shining. "I'm utterly flabbergasted," she told me. "I don't know whether I'm happy or not. But isn't it breathtaking? I'm like a child — I can hardly wait to get up there again, and look and look, and keep on discovering things. It's like finding that the Garden of Eden still exists."

"With no admittance," said Mac, sardonically. "Trespassers will be prosecuted."

"I just named that white rabbit," Tabby announced. "Abbott Rabbit. Isn't it beautiful?"

"It sounds nuts to me," said Roger.

Having to be careful of what was said before the children kept the conversation in safe channels. Mac said practically nothing, but I did my valiant best. I hung on to my headache as an excuse to go to bed early. I didn't want to be waiting for a chance to be alone with Mac, a chance that would never come now.

The Jays hadn't allowed their father to wait for the weekend. They brought him to the farm the next day when Mrs. Thornton was due home from the college; Mac had come in just before her, and a long day's painting in the hot sun hadn't improved his outlook on life.

He stood outside the group on the lawn, impassively watching while Miles Thornton (an older version of Josh with the same turquoise blue eyes, only behind glasses) handed Mrs. Thornton a portfolio of exquisite drawings. "Now, Madge, I'm sure that when you see these you'll want to be included. You and Mac study them while my junior partners show me whatever it is has them climbing the walls. Do you mind if I go up?"

"Of course not, Miles," Mrs. Thornton said. "After all, you're an heir, too."

Josh and June went with him, talking loudly and excitedly. The rest of us said nothing at all. Even the sun seemed to stand still in those few moments; we were caught in a web of time while we waited.

When Miles Thornton came from the house he was visibly moved. "Superb," he sighed. "Incredible, but there it is. A phenomenon."

"Has anyone found out anything about Grammie Angie?" Josh asked.

"I talked with Great-Uncle Matthew today," Mrs. Thornton said. "He says there's no evidence *against* Grammie Angie being Angela Mason. In the old Bible Joshua's wife's name is given as Angela M. Smith. M could be for Mason, and she could have dropped the Smith when she was painting professionally. Matthew was going over everything again today, and he and the others will be out tomorrow to see the room."

"Well, they'll all be happy to know the house will not be touched," said Miles Thorn-

ton. "There's no question about *that*. I'll re-
vise my projections to include the house
before I present the final version."

His smiled warmed and enlarged to beam
upon Mrs. Thornton like the sun. "In that
case, Madge, there'd probably be no objection
to your family living in the house, if you're
willing to show the room to people. At stated
hours, of course."

"Dad," said Josh, "if you found by accident a really spectacular emerald or dia-
mond, would you put it in a five-and-dime
setting? Or the most beautiful and suitable
one possible?"

"How about that, Dad?" June asked. Their
father looked severely at them.

"This should be discussed in private."

"Mac and his mother are part of the
family," Josh said. I stood up, but Josh put
his hands on my shoulders and gently pushed
me down again. He turned to face his father,
standing eye to eye with him.

"June and I don't think that anything
should be touched around here," he said. "The
whole farm is the setting. Everything is, as
far as you can see, and beyond. To cram the
place with buildings, mess up the lake with a
marina and outboards, destroy trees to put in
a golf course, even to tear down that barn
which is as strong as it ever was, would be an
inexcusable, unforgivable insult to that room
up there."

Mr. Thornton's blue eyes were as cold as
the shadows on snow. "How do you think I'm

going to sell *that* idea? Even if I wanted to? My heart's blood is in this project, and I thought some of yours was, too."

"Oh, Dad, the firm isn't going to rise or fall by this project," June protested. "You have plenty of business, because you're a super architect, and that's what we'll be, too, because we'll learn from you."

"Let me go before the gang," Josh said, "and I'll sell it to them, enough to make the difference. If they can bother to come all the way to New York in summer to chase up the big bucks, they can come out here and take a look at what they wanted to carve up sight unseen."

He looked around at me. "I know what *you're* thinking. That I was one of that bunch. Well, for everybody's information, I've had misgivings ever since I first came out here."

"And every time I looked at my day's photos," June said, "I remembered how it felt here when I was snapping them. But the project was so thrilling at first, and the idea of working with you, Dad, even before we finished college — it was all pretty exciting."

"Yeah," said Josh. "We tried not to let anything interfere. We got so we wouldn't even talk to each other about it, it was making us so uncomfortable. Working with you, Dad, is what I want. But not to tear up Hawthorne Farm or any part of it."

I don't know if anybody breathed. Even the little kids were awestruck without knowing why. Then Mr. Thornton reached for his portfolio and shut it up. "You two," he said softly. "All right, have a go at it. But remember, you can be outvoted. You'll be in the minority party."

"I like that already," said Josh. "More room to breathe. Do we get your vote?"

"If you'll give it to us," said June in a mock little-girl voice, "we'll never *ever* ask for another Christmas or birthday present."

"Honest?" Roger piped up, amazed. This broke the tension, and everybody laughed but Mac. He wasn't surrendering to hope yet.

"Are you eighteen, Mac?" Josh asked him. "That gives you a vote."

Mac shook his head.

"Sorry," said Josh, and he meant it. "Well, we'll get to work on all the other eighteens-and-over, starting tonight. Oh, first we'll convert our host, and then he'll offer his telephone free for The Cause."

"Well, come on," said June. "Don't stand there talking about it, let's get started!"

"I wish you all the luck in the world," Mrs. Thornton said fervently. She looked almost beautiful.

"You two go along," their father said. "I'll find a way back. I'm going to sit here and talk with Madge a while. Nobody can say that I don't lose gracefully."

Mac and I walked to the car with the Jays, and Josh and Mac shook hands. Mac wasn't effusive, but the handshake meant something. Afterwards we went down to the lake and pushed the canoe off into the water tinted rose and gold by the sunset. Luther and Leona Loon were singing duets again, and the mallard ducks talked among themselves.

Mac was still not talking. I knew what he was thinking. *What if our side doesn't win?* This uncertainty could be almost worse than being sure you'd lost. Because you can't help hoping, and all the time you're scared foolish. Even I, the optimist, was having a hard time with it.

Mrs. Thornton drove the Jays' father home that night to the Elliot Thorntons', and the next day those people came to see the room. They were certainly awed by it, and impressed, but didn't say right out how they'd vote. Of course all the Minority came — and came again. Great-Uncle Matthew was moved to tears. Roger and Tabby, who loved being tour guides, were disturbed by that.

"It's because the room is so beautiful," I told them, "and such a surprise."

Neighbors and townspeople showed up, and newspaper writers and photographers, even a television crew, from much farther away. (My father and mother drove out on a Sunday and stayed all day!) More Thornton heirs appeared, some from considerable distances. Josh and June escorted them, but Roger and Tabby insisted on taking them out to the cemetery, to Robin Hood's Oak, and the tree house. Behind their backs Josh made victory signs at me.

"Those kids are as good as the room," he

said. "Between them and the murals, everybody caves in. They ought to be at the meeting just to keep up the good work. Talk about psychological warfare. Who'd want to dispossess *them?*"

He and June never brought anyone out during lesson-time in the morning, and most other people called first to ask if it was all right to come. Mac was polite if he happened to be home, but he began working extra hours. How I missed the late afternoons with him, and those quiet evenings which I had first thought to be so deadly. So many callers drove in after dinner that Mac couldn't very well run away from all of them; wasn't he the man of the house?

Some days — *most* days — the only time we were alone was when we sat out on the back doorstep with the raccoons. I wanted to find out if he missed our private times together, but I didn't know how to say it. I wished he'd tell *me*. I'd have gone walking with him in the middle of the night if he'd asked me to, or got up at four in the morning for some dawn canoeing.

But he didn't ask me. I had to keep telling myself he was in such suspense about the fate of Hawthorne Farm that he couldn't let himself go. Maybe, too, he resented the Jays doing so much. Even when we kissed goodnight, he seemed to be thinking about something else. I couldn't really be mad, I was too sympathetic. But I missed him! I was hoping so hard for everything to come out right, and for us to be once more the way we used to be, that my mind ached.

As the time approached for the big meeting, and those heirs who lived as far away as the midwest and California were again gathering in New York, the Jays persuaded them to visit the farm. They arranged the transportation, and the Elliot Thorntons (now openly converted) would give them lunch. Between the Jays and the kids, they got a pretty thorough tour of the place.

Some could hardly wait to get away. "All very lovely, but these places belong to the past. Oh, save the house, if there's no way of removing the murals. *If* they're that priceless. The house could be the administration building. Remodel the interior. And bring it up to date, of course."

Others were very thoughtful. They walked alone back to the old cemetery, down to the lake, and climbed Strawberry Hill. They stood by the barn and watched the swallows.

"So this is where it all began," one woman said to me. "It's real to me now, for the first time. I'd like my children to come and walk around here."

There was one couple from California who had visited several times before, and Mrs. Thornton asked them to dinner. They were some of the original holdouts. "I don't get here as often as I'd like," the man said. "But I like knowing it's here. It's an oasis in a troubled world. It reminds us of what we were."

For these heirs it was not just the painted room. But the murals were the reason for many a pilgrimage that would not otherwise have taken place. And on that pilgrimage the pilgrims made great discoveries, not only in the world of Hawthorne Farm but in themselves.

N_ineteen_

Mrs. Thornton was going into New York for the vote, and she wanted Mac with her. Mrs. Hill would come over to stay the night with the kids and me.

I was determined we should have a little time together before he left, even for that short stay, and I schemed for it. He was going to put in a half day of work before coming home to clean up for the afternoon departure, and before I fell asleep the night before, I told myself to wake up *early*. So I did. I dressed in a chilly dawn, and crept downstairs without even a step creaking to give me away.

When Mac came down the back stairs, there I was in the kitchen with Walter. He looked surprised — not overjoyed — then grunted "Hi" and set about fixing his breakfast. I knew enough not to talk, but when he was ready to leave I got up and went out with him. "Walter, *stay*," I commanded, shutting the dog in the kitchen.

"I'm riding to the mailbox with you, Mac," I said calmly. "It's the only way we can manage any time alone these days. I hope you don't object."

He shrugged, and waited for me to climb in. "I guess I haven't been much company lately. Everything's so darned confused. So many people, so much yakking, and what's it all amount to?"

"Something good, I hope. You'll know by tomorrow night." The words gave me a cold shiver in my stomach.

"You *hope*?" he asked. "Aren't you sure? No feeling in your bones?"

"I don't trust that anymore." We were actually talking, and I'd have gladly ridden all the way to work with him and walked back from wherever it was, except that nobody at the farm would know where I was.

"As you say, by tomorrow night it'll all be over," Mac said, "and it'll be a relief, one way or the other. At least we'll be left in peace to figure out what to do next."

"Mac, do you still wish we hadn't discovered the room?"

"I don't know." He sounded perplexed. "I used to sound off about people wanting something they'd never seen. Well, the room, and the Jays' selling job, brought them out here in droves. But how many of them now think that the real estate is even better than they dreamed, and they can hardly wait for the bulldozers and chainsaws to take over?"

"And how many are now convinced that it would be a crime?" I said. "Besides the ones who always did think so?"

"We'll find out tomorrow," he said harshly, "how many are ready to give up their chance at some big money for an ideal. Or as some might put it, just to let Madge Thornton's kids have the place to themselves."

We were at the main road. I reached over, took his face in my hands and kissed him, and I jogged all the way back to the house.

Mrs. Thornton didn't go to work that day, and Mac came home at noon. By midafternoon they'd left in the stationwagon to pick up Great-Uncle Matthew and his wife and drive to New York, leaving the rest of us stranded high and dry while the tide of excitement went way, way out. I had this inner trembling from suspense, but I felt physically languid. Maybe from getting up so early. Nobody came, and we went down to the lake. The kids played and I read. Mrs. Hill drove herself in after supper. She hadn't seen the painted room yet, so the kids took her upstairs at once, and she was so fascinated that they stayed up there for an hour, all three of them talking a mile a minute.

Later she and I watched a spy movie on television, the first television I'd seen for weeks. It practically put me to sleep. I staggered up the stairs and went to bed without brushing my teeth, and slept as if I'd drowned. I even missed the rooster's crowing in the morning; the kids were up before I was.

Mrs. Hill had breakfast with us, made a chocolate layer cake, and went home. We did our chores, with me remembering how terrified I'd been when I was first left alone with the kids. Now I looked back at that Diana as if she were somebody else, a character in a book, perhaps. Certainly not today's Diana.

Well, we got through the morning. I tried not to think about New York. It would have been a help to be active a good distance away from the house, like hiking all the way around the lake, but I didn't want to leave the telephone. Somebody called from the village wanting to see the room and I told them to call again tonight. Otherwise, nothing happened until we were fixing our lunch.

The telephone rang and it was Mrs. Thornton. She and Mac had just left the meeting. "We won," she said quietly. "We're starting home as soon as we have something to eat."

"Fine," I said. That was the end of the conversation. I sat down limply on the stairs and Tabby ran to me. "Are you all right, Di? Are you sick?"

"Never better," I said, giving her a hug. "Your mother will be home tonight. Let's go eat."

They still hadn't any idea of what had been going on. Their mother and Mac had "business" in New York, that was all, and "business" meant nothing to them compared to their life at Hawthorne Farm. They were as innocent as Luther and Leona — they hadn't known of the terrible threat. And now they were safe.

I felt like crying. Instead I went upstairs during their quiet hour and sat on a trunk in the middle of the painted room, and looked at it for as long as I wanted to.

Mac will be happy now. That rang through my mind all the long afternoon of waiting. Everything around me looked different to me because it was safe, and it would look different to Mac because there would be no good-byes in his heart. *Mac will be happy now.*

In late afternoon I took a homemade chicken pie from the freezer and put it in the oven, and prepared a salad. The chocolate cake waited, rich and dark, on the counter.

Mac and Mrs. Thornton drove in before six. Walter and the kids greeted them joyously. The cats looked happy, too. If was if they had sensed the danger all along and now felt secure.

Mrs. Thornton had taken a little time to shop for small gifts for the children. For me there was a book of Emily Dickinson's poems.

"It's only a little thing, Di," she said, "as a token of our thanks for your part in all this."

I was touched and pleased, but I didn't protest, which always sounds silly. Mac had been smiling when they drove in, and now that the ice had been broken he couldn't seem to stop smiling. I could hardly wait until we were alone, when I could give him a big hug and get one back.

At dinner I heard all about the meeting, and the tentative plans for the farm. The idea was to make most of it into a legal nature preserve, which would help lower the taxes. As caretakers, the family would continue to live there, rent-free now, in exchange for showing the painted room at certain times. Mac would receive some financial help if necessary to get the farm moving again, when he finished his agricultural courses. There was also a suggestion that four or five simple cabins be built in unobtrusive spots, where other Thorntons could make visits and quietly enjoy the place. The kids were especially thrilled by this.

"Hey, wait up," Mac cautioned them. "If this happens, it won't be till next year." He grinned at me. "You should've heard Elliot. He acted as if he'd masterminded the whole thing. Practically had tears in his eyes. But the Jays had done the real work. Much as I hate to give 'em the credit," he added candidly. "They were coming back to Elliot's today, and yakking about us all having a victory celebration. And they're taking it for granted that they'll design the cabins." He didn't sound exactly miserable at the prospect. "I suppose we'll have to put up with them dropping in all the time now."

"You can afford to be generous," said his

mother. "Actually I've become very fond of them."

"And of Cousin Miles, too, I noticed," he teased her, and she twinkled back at him. The glum old Mac had disappeared.

Some neighbors drove in after dinner to offer congratulations, and Mrs. Thornton went out to sit on the lawn with them. The youngsters went to shut up the chickens, and Mac and I were alone at last.

Now I expected an embrace and a really fervent kiss to make up for all the absent-minded ones. But as I put down some dishes and turned to him, I met the strangest expression on his face. Was it embarrassment, or pity, or *what*? His eyes, green as his sports shirt under those peaked black eyebrows, looked long and somberly at me. His cheeks flushed.

"I'm sorry, Di," he said with obvious difficulty, "but I have to call Sharon."

"Why?" Shocked, I backed off.

"Because I drove her away in the first place. When all the bad stuff began to happen, I was worried and scared, but I wouldn't tell her anything. You know by now how I get. I can't help it." He moistened his lips. "I was rotten to her, and I've been rotten ever since. I just hope she hasn't gone for good."

"Well, it would serve you right!" I burst out. Then I tried to be dignified, and lowered my voice. "You've been thinking about her a lot lately, haven't you?"

"Yes. I'm sorry, Di. You've been great."

"Gee, thanks! That would look good on a gravestone, wouldn't it? 'She was great.' Or simply, 'Diana the Great'. Great *what*? Great idiot? Great patsy? Great wimp?"

He was very red. "I did care about you, Di. I wasn't lying!"

"No, you never did say you loved me. But I *thought* you did. I mean, I don't go around necking with just anybody, you know."

"I know that." He put his hand on my shoulder. "Did you love *me*?" he asked intensely. "Do you love me now?"

He had turned that blasted honesty of his right back on me. "Listen, Di, you were pretty lonesome when you came here, and then you were sorry for me and forgot about yourself. When I told you you were great, I meant it. You're a wonderful friend, a great comfort. I thought it might turn into something else if I worked at it."

"Because you thought you'd lost Sharon, right? And then she kept showing up. It would have helped all three of us a lot if you'd seen the light one of those times, instead of waiting until now."

"I couldn't," he protested. "I'd have kept on being rotten to her."

"Because you wouldn't let her in. You're selfish, Mac Thornton," I told him. "Bone selfish. You'll never hold onto anyone if you're going to lock yourself up and throw away the key every time something goes wrong." My voice broke. I waved my hand at the dirty dishes. "I'll do them — *alone* — after you make your call. Ask Sharon if she wants to babysit for the rest of the summer. You both want it that way, I'm sure."

I walked out of the house, hardly able to see where I was going. I wanted to be away from there so much I'd have started hitch-hiking if I dared. Which I didn't. So I went out across the meadow toward the woods, to hide out until I could go to bed without his mother thinking I was sick. In the morning I'd call home and ask them to come and get me. The darned dishes could wait forever as far as I was concerned.

Then I remembered something important. I ran for the house. Mrs. Thornton and her guests were still on the lawn as I dashed into the house, shouting, "Mac, you called her yet?"

"What?" he yelled from the front hall. He was sitting on the steps with the telephone.

"You talked to her yet?"

"She was out for a few minutes. I'm going to call right now."

"Don't offer her my job. I'm keeping it." I shoved my chin out at him. "For the kids and for your mother, and for me, too, a little. Not for *you*, so don't worry. You and Sharon have my blessing," I said haughtily.

As I turned away, blinking fresh tears, he said in a soft voice, "Di, I *am* sorry. I hope you can forgive me. I'm having a hard time forgiving myself. But I have to be honest, I can't be anything else. It's no good trying to live a lie."

I strode out with my chin up, but his last words stayed with me. *It's no good trying to live a lie.* And I knew I'd made the right decision. I'd be living a lie if I ran for home now; because I couldn't bear to let my parents or Kim know what had happened, I would have to be one terrific actress. And I just wasn't up to it.

Better to stay here where the little kids loved me and I loved them, and study like mad, while I suffered through the worst of it. Then I'd go home ready to start my life again. No one would guess my heartbreaking secret.

I could see me now. Sadder but wiser, with a gallant smile on my lips —

No! I couldn't see anything for the new spurt of tears. I headed blindly for the woods to curl up somewhere and howl as long as I wanted to without having to explain to anyone.

I stumbled into the woods, sat down with my back against a tree, and put my face onto my pulled-up knees. The birds were singing their evening songs, and the woods that used to frighten me felt safe and kind. Kinder than most people.

Something touched my head. Walter? I looked up and saw, through a blur of wet lashes, bright hair against the dark trees. Then Josh hunched down on his heels in front of me and took hold of my chin.

I feebly tried to pull free. "Go away. I look terrible."

"Not to me." He let go of my chin, and sat down beside me. "Here." He gave me a handkerchief. Not many boys carry freshly laundered handkerchiefs these days — smelling nice, too — but Josh Thornton's type would. I wiped my eyes and blew my nose, all pride gone.

He put his arm around me. "Now what's the trouble?"

"Nothing I can tell *you*."

"Why not? Whatever concerns you concerns me, Diana," he spoke soberly and quietly, "because I like you. I've liked you from the first time we met, when you were ready to defend Mac like a mother hen, and then the way you glared at me when I told you girls were no good at math." He chuckled. "It was fun to tease you, but the first time you looked at me as if you'd actually begun to like *me*, well, old Josh's stomach did a triple backward somersault. I guess it's a little more than just plain *like*."

I pulled back so I could look him in the face. "I don't believe it. You're only trying to cheer me up because Mac — because Mac —"

"Because with Mac it was Sharon all the time, right?" He wasn't smug or flip. "I know. I heard him on the telephone a few minutes ago, and you were disappearing into the woods. I could tell you were crying. So I chased you, and I didn't need Walter's help.

His mouth quirked up, but his blue eyes looked solemnly into mine.

We were silent for a few moments, just gazing at each other like that, and then he said very softly, "I'm going to be around here a lot this summer, Di."

"All right," I said.

"Listen to the thrushes," he said. "They know their woods are safe."

We sat with our backs against the old tree, his arm around me, listening to the flute-like songs in the trees as the dusk came on.

Suddenly I realized that I'd been attracted to Josh all along but I couldn't — or wouldn't — recognize it because I had to take Mac's side in the conflict. I had actually been relieved when he came over to our side so I could acknowledge to myself how much I liked him.

Just plain *liking* someone was an awfully good way to feel when you still had a lot of summer ahead of you. And whatever blossomed from that liking would come of itself, meant to be, not because I was sorry for him or myself. This time I wouldn't mistake pity or self-pity for love.